Coming Home to You

Robyn C Rye

Published by robyncrye, 2024.

Also by Robyn C Rye

Farnsworth Sisters
Marrying a Rogue
Rescuing Hannah

The Buckingham Sisters
Lady Maggie's Challenge
Layla's Unwanted Husband

The Evans Family
Sometimes Love is not Enough
Still the One
Moving Forward

Standalone
One More Chance
Lady Jayne's Reputation
Third Time's the Charm
Can't Stop Loving You

The Marriage Scam
An Unlikely Match
Searching For You
The Unexpected Suitor
The Lady and the Duke
Starting Over
An Unforgettable Stranger
The Duke's Revenge
The Temporary Wife
Against The Odds
Betrayed
No Good Turn Goes Unpunished
Lady Eloise's Soldier
Lillian's Forbidden Beau
Remember Me
Always Second Best
When One Door Closes
Coming Home to You
Chasing Shadows
Fool Me Once
Deserting Lady Audrey
My Unlikely Saviour
Lies and Deception
A New Beginning
Julia's Second Chance
The Hidden Enemy
The Maiden's Redemption
Miss Elizabeth's Season

Table of Contents

Copyright © 2024 by Robyn C Rye

Author's Message

As a reader, you may wonder why some words seem misspelt, but as an Australian writer, I use English spellings rather than American ones. So, NO! I am not a poor speller, and I have used the spell check, but with an Australian slant.

I loved recounting the story of Addison and Greyson, and I hope you enjoyed the unfolding tale of their trials and successes.

If you enjoyed the book and have a moment to spare, I would be grateful for a short review on the page or website where you purchased it. Your assistance in spreading the word is much appreciated. Reviews from readers like you make a massive difference in helping new readers discover stories like Coming Home to You.

Chapter One

Addison checked the bedroom to ensure Tyler hadn't left any belongings behind. As a foster mother, the most challenging part of the job was saying goodbye to someone you had nurtured and supported for weeks and sometimes months. While foster placements usually lasted longer, Addison's busy lifestyle led her to prefer acting as an emergency carer. Sometimes, when the calls came late at night, Addison feared for the mental well-being of children removed from an abusive or drug-related home, but she never refused the requests to take care of the children.

With a sigh, she closed the bedroom door; she would deal with the clean sheets and general tidy-up once Tyler was gone. This time, Addison hoped there might be a happy ending. Tyler's drug-addicted mother had spent months in rehab, and with her clean bill of health, the judge at the family court had given her custody of the ten-year-old boy. Addison walked into the lounge room, where the boy sat with his bag at his feet. Seating herself next to the boy, she said, "Tye, I hope everything works out with your mum, but if you need to talk, you can always ring me. I will never be too busy to listen to you, and if you need help, I can come to your aid."

The boy smiled and said, "Thanks, Addi. I hope it will be different this time, but now I know some people will care for me if Mum is not right. If it isn't okay with Mum, I won't wait so long to call for help."

Addison handed the boy a small cell phone.

"This is for you. My number is here. Hide the phone from your mum, even if you think things will be different. If things go badly and she finds out about the phone, it will be one of the things she will sell for cash. I will activate it for twelve months, but you will need to charge it periodically. Leave it turned off so it doesn't make any noises, and charge it when your mum is out of the house."

Tye hugged Addison. "Thanks, Addi, you're the best."

He slid the phone into his bag as someone knocked on the door. Addison smiled at the boy and said, "Well, it's time to go."

The person at the door was the regional coordinator, and she would take Tyler to meet his mum.

"Can I have a hug?"

Tye grinned and wrapped his arms around Addison.

"Stay safe, my friend," she said as the boy released her and turned to walk away. Stella, the regional coordinator, patted Addison on the arm and smiled sympathetically.

"I know parting is hard after spending months making a connection, but maybe it will work for Tyler this time."

"You're right; I'll keep my fingers crossed for them. I can't imagine how devastating it must be to have an addiction, and when the authorities take your child, that must be heartbreaking."

Once Stella and Tyler drove away, Addison decided to have a cuppa before she cleaned Tyler's room. The phone rang before she had made her drink, and it was her friend Cathy calling.

"Hi, Cath, what can I do for you?"

"It's what I can do for you. Has Tyler left? You probably need me to cheer you up. Meet me at Bean and Co., and we'll have decadent pastries and drinks."

"You know what? I was going to clean Tyler's room, but pastries win every time. What time?"

"Now, girlfriend. I'll meet you there."

Afternoon tea with Cathy was just what Addison needed. The two women taught at the same school, but Cathy taught the lowest grade, and Addison taught grade four. Almost immediately, the two women became firm friends. Cathy was one of the few teachers who didn't do her country service and move on. Because the school served the children from the army base, it was sometimes a hard slog. Addison didn't blame the children who had given up on education because being an army brat and relocating numerous times killed the desire to integrate into the community. She did her best to encourage the kids to participate and offered extra tuition for struggling students. The most frustrating part was reconnecting with the students; their parents had transferred, and the move destroyed all her excellent work.

Addison shook her head and focused on her friend. "Tell me about the book club you joined."

Addison laughed. "I diligently read the book, making notes where I felt the author did well or places that I thought she fell down and when I arrived at the house where the club was meeting, I discovered that not everyone was as diligent. Half of the women there hadn't read the book, and they said they used the club as an excuse to have a time out from their boring lives. Those ladies sure can drink."

"Oh. Will you go again?"

"Sure, it was a real hoot, and I need something in my life that makes me smile."

There was no better way to lift her spirits than to be with her friend, and Addison felt grateful that Cathy understood how hard it was for her to bid goodbye to her charges.

"Not wanting to hark back to school, but I had an interesting enrollment the other day."

"Interesting, good or interesting bad?"

Cathy screwed up her face. "Interesting, sad, is more like it. A little girl came in with an older man. The child has become the ward of the man's son. The soldier is on deployment somewhere, so rather than process her through the foster system, the big bosses decided the soldier's father would be a suitable guardian until the man returns home."

Addison nodded. "That sounds like a smart move."

"It might be smart if the man had an ounce of compassion about him. He orders this little girl around like she's a soldier, and considering that he was a career army officer, it's probably the only way he knows to talk to people. The little girl, Lacey, is terrified of him. She won't interact with the other kids and cries a lot."

"Have you tried talking to the man?"

"He says he's trying his best, but his best is woeful, truthfully."

"Thanks. Now, instead of stressing about how Tyler is going with his mum, I will be stressing about the little girl."

"Maybe you could check on her during your playground duty tomorrow."

After Addison arrived home, she didn't feel as sad as she had earlier, and that was all down to Cathy's intervention. She postponed cleaning Tyler's room and spent time in the kitchen preparing dinner. After placing the meal in the oven, Addison collected cleaning materials and sheets and headed to Tyler's room to clean and tidy. Addison was happy she had opted for a four-bedroom, two-bathroom option when looking for a house. In her role as an emergency foster carer, she assumed she would have to house a teenager at some point, and the extra bathroom would be a boon.

As she cleaned, Addison worried about the little girl Cathy described. The guardian might remain overseas for months, and the situation didn't sound sustainable for the little girl or the gruff ex-military man. Addison knew it wasn't her business to interfere; the thought of the little girl suffering for months until her guardian returned didn't sit well with her. On Monday, when she returned to school, Addison decided to do as Cathy suggested: check on the little girl and see if she could devise a resolution.

Having decided to investigate the situation with the little girl, Addison finished cleaning the room. She bundled the sheets into the washing machine with towels, teatowels, and washcloths. The washing machine seemed to take ages to work through its cycle, but Addison hoped to have the laundry hung out before sitting down for dinner. With little else to do, she poured herself a glass of wine, grabbed her book and sat down to read and relax.

The following day, Addison prepared a picnic and headed out of town, driving to the Clarence waterfalls and picnic ground. She considered calling Cathy, but knew her friend had visited her parents at their home an hour from Chessberry. During the school holidays and the summer, the area was popular with families, but fewer people flocked to the reserve as autumn drew nearer. Today, Addison had the area to herself, except for a few brave souls who dabbled in the pool that ran from the waterfalls. Leaving her picnic in the car, Addison hiked along a trail she knew would bring her to the other side of the falls. The area was picturesque, with its clean air, soothing water sounds, and chirping birds that relaxed Addison. However, no matter how hard she tried to push the thought aside, the plight of the little girl, Cathy, who was known as Lacey, lingered in the back of her mind.

Chapter Two

O n Monday morning, Addison opened the classroom door and struggled inside, juggling her books and bag. Schools had a particular smell; a combination of bodies, books, and chalkboards added to the aroma in the older schools. Addison wrinkled her nose, and after depositing her load on the nearest desk, she hurried to open the windows.

Once the students arrived, Addison greeted the children and chatted with the parents, who escorted their offspring to the classroom. Most parents allowed their children to take themselves to class at the grade four level, but if a parent had a concern or a request, it was easier to discuss the issues before class, and Addison was accommodating. The bell signalled the need to assemble outside, and the parents and children dispersed. The children lined up by grade level, and Addison tried to find the girl Cathy had described, but from her vantage point, she couldn't see her.

After entering the room with her students, Addison's day moved on quickly; before she knew it, lunchtime had arrived. Twice a week, each teacher supervised the students in the playground, and today was Addison's first shift. Moving from area to area to keep a visible presence to deter any bad behaviour, Addison finally saw the sad girl. The child sat in a corner of the undercover area, crying. Addison approached the girl, and the child watched as she advanced. Squatting down so she wasn't looming over the child, Addison said,

"Why are you so sad?"

The child shrugged and looked down, but she remained mute despite what Addison said. Not wanting to harass the child, Addison moved away, but the little girl's sad face and dishevelled appearance tugged at her heart.

In the afternoon, Addison had a spare period because her class were at music, so she didn't have to remain in her room to dismiss the class.

As she walked towards Cathy's class, she wondered if she ought to mind her own business, but the memory of the sad little girl pushed her on. Standing outside the classroom, she attempted to identify the man that Cathy said had no empathy, and when Lacey emerged from the room, she cringed as a man walked towards her. The man appeared to be in his fifties or sixties and had an air of command. When he spoke to the girl, it was more a bark than an instruction, and as he reached to guide her towards the exit, Lacey flinched when he touched her. Addison watched as the pair left the school, and when Cathy's students had departed, she went inside to talk to her friend.

"Cath, I just saw your sad child, and we need to act. Her guardian's father might not be a bad man, but he is traumatising the child so badly that I believe she will be a zombie by the time her guardian arrives."

"What can we do?"

"Can you ask him to meet me in my room after school tomorrow? I'm not sure what to suggest, but in good conscience, I can't watch that little girl suffer."

Addison second-guessed her decision as she sat in her room, waiting for the man to arrive. Cathy told her his name was Major Pelleser and that he lived around the corner from the school. The footsteps sounded like they were marching as the man approached. His gruff voice scolded the little girl as they arrived at Addison's classroom. When she invited him to enter, the man looked around in confusion.

"Why am I in this room, and who are you to request a meeting with me?"

"I am Addison Bradley, and I want to discuss something with you. Before we do, let me set Lacey up with an activity."

The man glared at Addison with displeasure, but she ignored him until she encouraged Lacey to use the pencil set out before her to draw a picture.

"Major Pellesser, I am concerned about Lacey's mental welfare. She is sad, never mixes with the other children and rarely speaks. I understand that your son was named guardian by Lacey's late mother, but it must be hard for you to foster a small child for an undetermined time."

The man sighed. "I'm doing my best, but when I was in the army, I was often away on courses or deployment, and my wife raised our children. We had three sons, so I don't know what to do with a minor female child. It feels wrong to help her bathe or dress, and I know she is afraid of me. The child protection people thought settling her with me was the proper agreement, but I doubted the validity of the option then and with every day that passes, the choice grows steadily worse."

Addison glanced over where Lacey sat with her pencils moving across the page.

"Major Pellesser, I am an accredited foster carer and generally take on emergency cases until suitable accommodation becomes available. While we don't want to place Lacey in the foster system, I could act as her carer until your son returns if that would suit you."

The man narrowed his eyes. "What's in it for you?"

"The relief of not watching Lacey's heartbreak every day."

Major Pellesser nodded. "If you take the child, I will pay for any outstanding costs for her, but how do we do this?"

"Give me some time alone with Lacey, and then I can collect her belongings from your place. Does your son know of his friend's death and the guardianship of Lacey?"

"No, I'm not much of a letter writer."

"Perhaps if you have an address, I could notify him of his friend's death and what that means for him. It would be unwise to have him arrive to discover he had a six-year-old girl as his responsibility."

The relief on the face of the Major was evident, and Addison wondered how he could run a regiment if he couldn't put his hand up and ask for help.

When Major Pellesser left the room, Addison approached Lacey. The child laid down her pencil and looked at Addison with concern. In a gentle voice, Addison said, "Lacey, come here to me."

Watching the child's hesitation hurt Addison, but she had to have the child's permission before she touched the child or changed her living arrangements. Addison held out her hand, and like a timid animal, Lacey took it.

"Lacey, I am Miss Bradley. It must be confusing to have people you don't know take it upon themselves to change your school and home. Your mother chose a friend she trusts to be your guardian, but that's currently impossible as he is overseas. Major Pellesser is trying his best, but we both know his best is not good enough. Would you like to live with me until your guardian returns from overseas?"

Lacey looked at Addison with fearful eyes.

"Will you yell at me?"

"No, but there is something I think you need now. Did your mum give you good hugs?"

Lacey's eyes teared up, and she sobbed as she said, "Yes, but she got sick, and then Mrs Francis wouldn't take me to see her anymore."

"I'm sure Mrs Francis was doing what she thought was best because sometimes it is better to remember the person you loved when they were well and not when they are so sick that they look dreadful. Lacey, I'm not your mum, but I give pretty good hugs. Would you like a hug?"

Lacey hesitated for a moment and then walked into Addison's arms. The weeping became wrenching, and Addison held on tight as the little girl cried.

Eventually, Lacey's sobs subsided, and she extracted herself from Addison's hug.

"My mummy died, and I don't want to live with that man."

Addison and Lacey drove to the Major's house to collect Lacey's belongings.

"There are some boxes that the neighbour packed, but they can stay here for now."

Lacey tugged at Addison's arm and whispered. "Please bring the boxes. Barney is in there somewhere."

Unaware of who or what Barney was, Addison made a snap decision.

"Major, we will take the boxes. It might take a few trips, but it would be comforting for Lacey to have some familiar belongings. Let's take as many as possible on the first trip because I will have to put the child's car seat in the back when we get home, limiting the number we can carry."

Removing the boxes was time-consuming, and one of them was extremely heavy.

"How will you manage once you get these boxes home?"

"I have a trolley, and I'll use that. Hopefully, we'll be all right."

Once Addison moved the boxes from the car to the lounge room, she said, "I guess you're keen to open the boxes, but do you need a snack first? It might take a while to find Barney."

After they finished their sandwich and drink, Addison used a Stanley knife to slit the tape on the boxes' lids. They unpacked one box at a time. Lacey looked as though she had discovered a treasure. The kind Mrs Francis had included some of Lacey's mother's clothes, photos, and ornaments. By the time they opened the last box, the contents of the others strewn around them, Addison feared Barney was not in the boxes but had been lost. Lacey's loud shout of "Barney" relieved Addison. Having your life turned upside down and having your special toy misplaced would be a massive source of stress for the child.

"We will decide where to put your favourite things tomorrow, but it might be time to bathe before tea. Come into your bedroom, and we'll find your pyjamas. If you put Barney on the sink, he will stay dry."

There were so many things Lacey needed, and tomorrow, Addison intended to put the Major to the test by buying Lacey a school uniform, a backpack and other school items. Eventually, she planned to buy Lacey some new clothes, but for now, she would let her hold onto familiar things.

Addison did what the Major couldn't do and supervised Lacey's bath. She washed her young charge's hair, and once they had eaten tea, Addison plugged in a night light for Lacey and plopped down on the bed to read the little girl a story. Clutching Barney, Lacey listened to the story, but fatigue caught up with her, and she closed her eyes before the story ended. Addison tucked the blankets around her new charge and left the room.

The immediate task for Addison was more difficult than looking after a small girl. An email would have been faster, but the Major didn't have his son's email address, which made Addison wonder about the family dynamics. Where would the mother and other children be if the man had sons? Writing a letter to a man she didn't know to inform him of the death of his friend was challenging, but notifying him of his new charge required tact. After two drafts, Addison decided the draft was as good as she could get it and found an envelope for postage. The man would get her letter one way or another, and they could go from there.

The following day, Addison stopped at the post office to send the letter, unsure how long delivery would take, considering it had to be rerouted to wherever Greyson Pellesser was stationed. When she dropped Lacey off at school, the little girl acknowledged her teacher and sat down on the mat to look at a picture book. Cathy raised her eyebrows, and after Addison said goodbye to Lacey, the women went outside to discuss her.

"Tell me what happened at your meeting with the Major."

"The man admitted he was struggling and considered returning to child services to ask to place her in a foster home until his son returned. I couldn't let that happen because Lieutenant Pellesser would have to jump through hoops to release her once the department officially placed her. Depending on the home, Lacey would be no happier than in her current situation. We agreed for me to be her primary carer until the son returns."

"Who will pay for her upkeep?"

"The Major promised to repay me for anything I buy and a weekly stipend for her food. I'm glad I did this because she was grieving her mother, and the one thing that would comfort her was a ragged old bear she called Barney. When the Major said there were boxes a neighbour packed, I insisted on taking them with me because Lacey was sure Barney was in one of the boxes, and she was right."

The electronic bell's ringing ended their discussion, but they agreed to catch up at the end of the day to review Lacey's progress. Now that Lacey was speaking, Cathy had a better chance of discovering what Lacey knew.

Chapter Three

"**M**ail for you, Lieutenant. Someone loves you."

Greyson ignored the grinning face of the corporal who handed him the letter and looked curiously at the envelope. The name on the back didn't ring any bells, and it was evident by the battered state of the letter that it had been diverted more than once. With the corporal hanging around to look at the letter, hopefully, Greyson glared at the man and sent him on his way. Privacy, while deployed, was a scarce commodity, but Greyson was not going to allow the other man to peek at his mail before he digested its contents.

To Lieutenant Greyson Pellesser,

Dear Greyson,

Your father gave me your address because there is news you need to hear before you return home.

I regret to inform you that your childhood friend, Tammy Fisher, died recently after a long battle with cancer. During her hospitalisation, Tammy had little support and relied on the kindness of an elderly neighbour. Your friend left everything she owned — little more than photos and mementos — to her six-year-old daughter.

Before Tammy died, she wrote a will nominating you as the child's guardian. Lacey is in my care for the time being. I would appreciate a faster way to communicate with you. I have included my email address and mobile number for you to contact me. I know that the news of your new ward will stun you, but with no relations, I assume Tammy didn't want her daughter to become a ward of the state. The little girl is traumatised by what has happened, and I hope that by the time you meet her, she will be in a better state.

Regards

Addison Bradley

Greyson read and re-read the letter, hoping that somehow he had misread it, but no —apparently he had become the parent of a six-year-old daughter. The news that Tammy died alone and of cancer made him regret not keeping in touch with her. His guilt at being a poor friend would trouble him for some time, and the knowledge that she thought of him when she was dying humbled him. Tammy naming him as her daughter's guardian was a sad indictment of her parents, whom she had fallen out with when she left for college, particularly as the letter said she died alone. Dear God, what did he know about raising a child? Greyson had given up any thoughts of having a wife and child at age thirty. After being an army brat himself, he wouldn't condemn another child to move from city to city, all the while being the new kid at school and rarely making friends before the next move came.

Greyson had to make sense of the news before he emailed or texted the carer. Who was the woman who sent the letter, and why was she caring for Tammy's daughter if she said Tammy died alone? If there was no one else to care for the child, did that mean he should cancel any hope of promotion or leave the army entirely? He wanted to discuss his dilemma, but didn't want the news to circulate in the camp. With the letter tucked back into the battered envelope, Greyson walked along the walkway and knocked on the door of the Captain's office. The man was gruff, but he could listen and sometimes offer advice. Looking up with a scowl, the man said, "What can I do for you, Grey?"

"I have an unusual situation I want to discuss with someone, and even if you can't give me advice, I know that whatever I tell you won't do the rounds of the camp."

The Captain sat back in his chair and said, " Okay, let's hear about your situation."

As Greyson related the content of the letter and the stunning news that he was now the guardian of a six-year-old girl, the Captain's eyebrows rose.

"You're not wrong about the difficulty this poses. As the child's guardian, can you ask the court to make her a ward of the state? She will have a foster family, and you can continue your career."

"Knowing that Tammy nominated me as the guardian so she didn't go into the foster system would cause me guilt."

"What about the woman looking after her now, or even trying to contact the grandparents? They may have fallen out with their daughter, but surely they would welcome a granddaughter."

"Yeah, that might work. I don't know where the old biddy who is caring for her now comes into the equation, and seeing as Dad let her tell me about Tammy, I doubt he will answer my questions even if I bother asking."

"There's only one way to get answers. You will have to email the woman and ask some questions."

"You're right, but I needed someone else's take on things. Thanks, Captain."

After saluting his superior, Greyson strolled back to his tent, his problem filling his thoughts.

Email from Greyson

Greetings, Miss Bradley.

I was saddened and stunned by your letter, which, according to the date, has been in the system for three weeks, which explains the delay in contacting you. Before I go any further, I have questions regarding Lacey Fisher's care. Who are you, and how are you involved in caring for Lacey? You say Tammy died without anybody to support her, so if she trusted you to care for her child, why weren't you there in her darkest hour, and why are you not the girl's guardian?

As a serving army officer, my life is hardly conducive to bringing up a child, and while I don't want to place her in the foster system, I will hire an investigator to locate the grandparents. Tammy and her parents were estranged; I can't imagine them not stepping up once they realised Lacey needed her family.

My deployment ends in three months, so I will reassess my options if the situation isn't resolved by then.

Regards

Greyson Pellesser.

Happy with his email, Greyson hit send and began his hunt online for a private inspector. The problem seemed impossible when he first read the letter, but the solution was more straightforward than Greyson imagined.

When Addison heard the alert on her phone, she decided to read the reply on her computer, waking the sleeping machine. As she read, her heart sank. Addison wasn't sure if she was angry or sad that the man intended to pass off his responsibilities to grandparents who couldn't support their daughter as she lay dying. She expected questions regarding her and how she became Lacey's carer, but the insinuation that she hadn't supported a woman she didn't know rankled. His suggestion that he hire a private investigator encouraged Addison to use her contacts in the foster system to speak to the woman who cared for Lacey once her mother went into the hospital. Indeed, the neighbour might have more information about Tammy's background, and if so, they could avoid an uncomfortable situation if the parents weren't the solution Greyson hoped they were.

Addison checked the time on her PC and realised it was too late tonight to call people, but tomorrow, when Lacy went to her first guides meeting, Addison would use that alone time to call in favours. She knew she had to respond to Greyson's email, especially since she had requested a quicker way to reach him. However, Addison decided to delay her reply until she had spoken with Mrs Francis. Hopefully, the woman wouldn't be too hard to track down.

Her first point of contact was Stella.

"Addison, good to hear from you. Are you ringing about Tyler, or can I help you with something else?"

"Of course, I want to know how Tyler is going, but I have another problem that I need help with."

"First, I'll tell you about Tyler, and then you can inform me about your problem. When I dropped Tyason off with his mother, he was a little wary because she was abusive when he lived there, as you know. But I stayed for an hour or two, and they seemed to be doing well. I have a welfare check booked for late next week, and I will continue to do those, time permitting, until they reach the one-year mark. Now, what is your problem?"

As Addison explained about Lacey, Stella made affirmative noises.

"I'm sorry the man we settled her with was so wrong, but it made sense on paper. The grandparents are a good idea, although I wonder why they haven't stepped up, because the police notified her parents of the woman's death. When they refused to respond, the authorities buried the poor woman in a pauper's grave. That doesn't sound like anyone I would ask to raise a child."

"That was my concern, and Greyson may find the grandparents, but just because they are kin doesn't make them suitable. I thought the person who could tell me more about the family dynamic was the woman who looked after Lacey before child services got involved."

"Okay, give me a minute to bring up the report. Will you visit in person or talk on the phone?"

" I'll visit."

Addison now had the woman's address who had called child services about Lacey, and she needed to organise a trip. Would taking Lacey with her be too traumatic for the girl, or would she enjoy seeing the neighbour? After the school day finished, Addison went to Lacey's classroom to speak to Cathy. Addison sat Lacey at a computer with learning games on the screen and moved Cathy aside so she could ask her about the trip.

"I have the address of Mrs Francis, Lacey's neighbour. Do you think I should take her with me, or do you think it would be too traumatic to visit her former home?"

"Do you think Lacey would stay with me? Returning to where she and her mother lived might bring back bad memories, and she has made so many gains since she moved in with you; it would be a pity to put that in jeopardy."

So, three days after locating Mrs Francis, Addison left Lacey with Cathy and travelled to Heidelberg. As Addison approached the outskirts of the town, her nerves kicked in. What if the woman couldn't answer any questions, and she had to rely on Greyson's investigator to turn up answers? Her GPS directed her to a run-down area with old houses and apartments. Tammy Fisher and Lacey lived in a flat on the second storey, and the neighbour lived next door. Addison braced herself; would the woman be forthcoming? Mrs Francis opened the door with a smile and said, "You must be the lady who is caring for Lacey. Foster care rang me to tell me that you were coming."

"Ah, good, I'm glad they did."

"Come in and tell me how little Lacey is going."

Addison followed the woman inside, and once they sat in the kitchen with drinks, she said,

"The Child Protection staff decided Major Pellesser could mind Lacey until her guardian returns from his deployment. Not only was she sad, but she was terrified of the man because he treated her like one of his soldiers and barked instructions at her. Thankfully, he agreed to my taking Lacey into my home, and she is coming on in leaps and bounds."

Addison told the woman that the staff had made a decision with the best intentions, but it had turned into a disaster.

Mrs Francis nodded. "I only saw that man briefly and knew he would scare that poor child. I'm glad he recognised that he wasn't equipped to deal with a little girl and surrendered her to you."

"I have some questions to ask, and please forgive me if I seem nosy. Recently, I received an email from the man Tammy chose as Lacey's guardian. He understands the responsibility but wants to pass it off to someone else. I don't blame him for shying away from the task. Not many single thirty-year-old males want to become the guardian of a child they haven't met."

"No, I assume it came as a shock. Tammy said she hadn't seen him for years but knew he was a kind and decent man when she knew him."

"Greyson, the guardian, said Tammy's parents threw her out of the house when she became pregnant. Did she ever reach out to them when it became obvious that she was terminal?"

"Over the years, Tammy had reached out to them on many occasions. She tried when Lacey was born and numerous times after that. She contacted them when her illness became debilitating, and she had to stay in the hospital, but her parents never responded."

"How did you become Lacey's carer?"

"I could have rung the authorities, but Tammy begged me not to let them take her. That's when she wrote a will asking the soldier to be Lacey's guardian."

"Do you think Tammy's parents would take Lacey into their home, considering the circumstances?"

"I don't know, but having mistreated Tammy, do you believe they would be loving and kind to the proof of their daughter's disgrace?"

Addison nodded. "That was my concern when Lieutenant Greyson suggested finding the grandparents. I guess Tammy didn't tell you about Lacey's father?"

Mrs Francis said, "A little bit, but not his name. She said she was pregnant before she realised he was married."

"I wonder if one of those DNA sites they advertise on telly to find long-lost ancestors would turn up a relative?"

"You care for her, don't you? If the soldier doesn't want her, maybe you could adopt her?"

Addison laughed. "It might come to that. Fostering children always leaves the carer open to becoming too attached. The adoption route sounds viable in a case like this one, where no parents or relatives exist, but the problem is that there are so many needy children that a carer could end up like the rhyme of the old lady who lived in a shoe."

Mrs Francis laughed.

"I'm sure you'll think of something."

"Oh, I meant to say thank you for the things you boxed up. While Lacey was with the Major, she was too scared to ask him to find Barney, but when she came to me, we unpacked the boxes and found the things you kindly packed. Lacey was relieved to find Barney, so thanks."

"It was the least I could do for them. I would suggest that in time, you could take Lacey to see her mother's grave, but the authorities interred Tammy in a pauper's grave, so it might be better not to go there."

"I didn't know the lady, but it seems that life was not kind, and except for you, her friends abandoned her as they moved on with their lives. I wonder whether Greyson Pellesser feels guilty when remembering his childhood friend. According to Major Pellesser's recollection, they were inseparable as children and teenagers, and lost touch after he joined the army. However, they must have had some initial contact, since he knew Tammy was estranged from her parents.

"Sometimes losing touch is inevitable. I was glad I was able to help."

"This might not be my place, but if I give you my phone number and you need help, please don't hesitate to call me."

Mrs Francis patted Addison's hand. "Thank you, dear. You are a kind soul; don't let the world take advantage of you."

Chapter Four

W hen Addison collected Lacey from Cathy's house, she gave her friend a run-down of what Mrs Francis had told her.

"Why don't you do the ancestry thing? Even if you don't find someone who wants to be her guardian, having relatives who share your gene pool in the future might be helpful."

"Yeah, I can do that, but regardless of what happens there, she can't go to the grandparents. I'd better get her home, and tonight, I'll email Greyson."

Addison knew that what she had to tell Greyson about the grandparents would not please him, and she understood his desire to keep this turn of events from impacting his life, but when Lacey's future was in his hands, she wished he would be brave and consider the child, not just himself. Addison composed the email and sent it off, knowing the next move was in Greyson's court.

Dear Grayson,

Sorry for the delay; I was doing some investigation of my own. Now, to answer your questions. I am a teacher at Lacey's current school, and I rescued her from your father. The child protection staff decided that, as you were named her guardian, your father could step in until you returned. Every time I saw her, she was crying, and when your father arrived to collect her, she cringed and began to shake. Unable to watch their distress any longer, I approached your father, who admitted he was in over his head. He knew Lacey was frightened by his loud voice and the commands he issued, but he didn't know what to do. You've never seen a more relieved man than he was when I offered to care for Lacey until your return.

I have foster care qualifications, but have taken Lacy as a favour to your father. I had never met Tammy, so I am offended that you would suggest I failed in my duty to her as a friend. (Have you looked in the mirror?)

Today, I spoke to Mrs Francis, the woman who minded Lacey when Tammy went into the hospital, and she said Tammy had reached out to her parents numerous times and, the last time, told them of her condition and begged them for help. They never responded, so even if you find the grandparents, they are unlikely to take Lacey into their home, and if they did, I would be concerned that they would take their anger out on her. Call your investigator off, Lieutenant. The grandparents are not an option. Your friend is buried in a pauper's grave because her parents would not claim Tammy's body. That is the kind of people you hoped might care for Lacey.

Even if we come up with a solution that suits us all, may I suggest that you make some FaceTime calls so that Lacey can see the man her mother remembered on her deathbed?

Regards

Addison Bradley.

Greyson read the email with annoyance. The damn woman had just blown his one option out of the water, and now she wanted him to FaceTime with the child. Did she have any idea of the difficulty the deathbed request placed him in? He had no time in his life for a child; her making him feel guilty was wrong. He imagined the teacher with foster authorisation was some old biddy who was busy sticking her nose into something that wasn't any of her business. Greyson knew his father was gruff, but why would he relinquish the child to a busybody who thought she knew better?

As he stewed about the email, a knock on the door drew him away from his computer. A young corporal saluted him and delivered a message from the Captain to come to his office at his earliest convenience. After closing his laptop, Greyson thanked the messenger and headed to the Captain's office. When he arrived at the office, after saluting the man, he sat in the chair near the desk and said, "What can I do for you, sir?"

"You seem distracted lately, and I'd guess it has something to do with the child's guardianship."

Greyson nodded.

"The old biddy who is minding the child says she saved her from my father. I know the man can be stern, but he isn't unkind. She also investigated the grandparents, and according to her sources, Tammy had attempted to reconcile with her parents on multiple occasions. When she was diagnosed with cancer, she contacted them, begging for assistance, but they never replied. The parents wouldn't claim Tammy's body, and she is buried in a pauper's grave. The woman says that the grandparents aren't an option because if they took the child, they might well take out their anger on their daughter or the child, and I fear she might be right."

"Hmm. You are in a bind. It appears foster care may be your only option."

"The woman wants me to FaceTime the kid, even if I decide not to agree to become her guardian, because Lacey needs to meet the man her mother trusted enough to ask him to care for her."

"That shouldn't be hard to organise; meeting the girl might help you decide what to do about her."

"I'll text the woman to make time and move on from there. I doubt meeting the child online will help me decide what to do. My lifestyle is not conducive to having kids."

The Captain nodded his agreement but said, "Other members of the force manage with a wife and children. I'll concede that there are many broken marriages when spouses get too lonely to stay faithful, but even then, the soldiers manage to accommodate their kids."

"Yeah, well, that won't be me."

When the text message arrived with a time for the call, Addison talked to Lacey about what would happen. She suggested they consider some questions to ask the man to make the call less awkward. If the call went well, Addison might suggest making it a fortnightly or weekly occurrence, but not knowing Greyson's schedule, she wasn't sure if this was possible. Addison hoped that Greyson didn't let his aversion to the task he had inherited seep into the conversation.

Before her conversation with Greyson, Addison investigated the ancestry website to learn what she needed to do and how to find Lacey's relatives. She wasn't hopeful that a long-lost relative would offer to take Lacey. If they did, Addison would be cautious about placing the little girl without investigations and checking financial details. Addison hoped Lacey might connect with cousins or other relatives as she grew older. For the moment, she wasn't letting Greyson know what she had done in case he latched onto that as a way of divesting himself of the unwelcome inheritance he was gifted.

The time for the call arrived, and Addison sat Lacey in a chair in the room she used as her study. The light in the room was intense as no blinds or curtains covered the window. When the phone rang, Lacey and Addison looked at each other with delight. Addison pressed the button, filling the screen with a man's face. The man smiled and introduced himself to Lacey, who responded with her name.

Addison stayed out of the picture but close by so she could hear the conversation, and when it stalled, she coached Lacey on what to say next. The time went fast, and when Greyson said he had to go, Lacey said, "Can you talk to me again? I want to hear about my mum when she was little." Addison was delighted when he agreed and said he would text her for the date of the next call.

Lacey was happy after talking to Greyson and said, "I was scared he was like his dad, but he is quiet and smiles."

Addison nodded. Addison could see the soldier from where she stood while the two talked, although she tried to stay out of range of the cameras so he couldn't see her. The soldier's quiet voice and questions gave Addison hope that he might come to like Lacey if they continued to talk, and the outcome might be more positive.

Addison sent Lacey in to put on her pyjamas and clean her teeth, and she texted Greyson while the little girl was busy.

Thanks for the call. Lacey is less worried about meeting you. I explained that she mightn't live with you, but she looks forward to hearing more about her mum.

Chapter Five

"Lacey, did you belong to any sporting clubs when you lived with your mum? Is there something you would like to try?"

"Maria at school says she goes to Guides. She says they do fun things; can I try that?"

"You sure can. Let me find out where the group meet and what you need."

A few days later, after Addison dropped Lacey off at Guides, she and Cathy met at the local coffee shop. Cathy had many questions about the call, and Addison was happy to share the information.

"So you didn't see him?"

"No, I wanted him to focus on Lacey, so I stayed out of the picture. I could see a little bit of him; he was clean-shaven with a square chin and full lips, but I have no idea what he looked like after that. It's a bit like wearing a mask, but in reverse. The screen covered the top half of his face instead of covering the bottom part."

"Will he call again before he comes home?"

"Maybe, I don't know. But let me tell you what I did."

As Addison related her web search and the process she went through to register Lacey's DNA on the programme, Cathy clapped her hands.

"So much for the soldier! You one-upped him in the parents' investigation, and now you're potentially finding relatives for Lacey. Would you let her go if you found someone willing to take Lacey?"

"I'm not sure. It depends on the person, and it's not up to me. Whatever happens to Lacey has to be approved and signed off by Greyson."

The weeks crawled by, punctuated by video calls from Greyson and days at school. What had started as a fortnightly thing had evolved into weekly calls, and Lacey looked forward to them. She was confident and open with Greyson, and Addison wondered if she would retain that confidence when faced with the man in the flesh.

After his latest call, his mate Slater, who had initially helped set it up, said, "Have you ever seen the teacher?"

Greyson looked confused.

"Why would I want to meet some old hag who virtually kidnapped my ward from my father?"

"Mate, I've met your father, and he terrified me; I can imagine what effect he had on a grieving six-year-old. Maybe you should thank the woman for saving your father and the little girl. And as for an old bag, I've listened to a few of those calls, and when she prompts the girl or answers a question, her voice sounds like a young woman's. I don't know why you thought she was old, but I'll bet she's not."

Greyson shrugged.

"I can ask her to appear on screen next time, but if she isn't old, she must be ugly. Why else would she avoid the camera?"

Slater laughed. "I'll bet you a twenty she isn't ugly. Just because she is kind enough to look after your ward doesn't mean she's ugly. And she might avoid the camera, so your attention is on the girl."

Greyson held out his hand. "A twenty it is."

Lacey eagerly waited for Wednesday because that was when Greyson would call, but she had to get through the week first. Addison congratulated herself on enrolling Lacey in Guides because being with other girls, both older and younger, helped Lacey make friends. Their activities were exciting and enjoyable, and Lacey loved her new uniform. Fitting in with those around her was essential, and Major Pellesser kept his word. He paid for Lacey's school uniform and the Guides' outfit without any fuss. Addison talked with Lacey about joining Little Aths or a soccer team, but her girl was trying to build the confidence to try one. Addison didn't push; she suggested the ideas and waited for Lacey to decide when she was ready.

"Lacey, why don't you wear your Guide uniform? You can show Greyson when he calls."

When the phone rang, Lacey was ready and dressed in her outfit to show Greyson. As Greyson and Lacey talked, Addison could hear someone in the background. Usually, Greyson had the room to himself, so distractions from other people weren't an issue. Halfway through the call, Greyson sighed.

"Lacey, is there a reason I haven't seen your teacher? Does she look like Shrek, and is she too shy to show her face?"

Lacey giggled. "She doesn't look like Shrek; she is beautiful."

"I don't believe you. Ask your teacher to stand where I can see her."

He heard her voice, and a moment later, a woman sat down with Lacey in her lap. She smiled at him and said, "I might not be beautiful, but I don't look like Shrek either."

She heard another man say, "Holy moly, Grey, I win, you lose."

"Ah, who is that, and what was the bet?"

Greyson looked ashamed.

"That's my mate, Striker, and he asked why you never show your face. I guessed it was because you were ugly, and he bet me twenty dollars that you weren't. It's clear he wins."

Addison laughed and said, "I already like your friend."

Now that Addison had revealed her face, she contributed to weekly conversations. Having not seen all of Greyson's face, Addison was pleased that his visage was as pleasing as his attitude with Lacey. The more the three talked, the more they learned about each other. Addison generally texted Greyson after Lacey went to bed, and she found the conversation amusing and thought-provoking. Lacey's placement after Greyson returned to Australia was the one topic they never discussed. Addison fretted about what would happen to the little girl, but no amount of worry could solve the problem.

As the days passed, Lacey grew more confident in her interactions with others, although occasionally, something would remind her of her mother, and she would become weepy and sad. Addison knew that the unhappy days were inevitable. She continued to support Lacey, telling her that grief was an emotion like happiness, and as she didn't ignore things that made her happy, she shouldn't ignore things that made her sad.

Feeling stuck in a rut and not wanting to breeze through the week waiting for Wednesday, Addison decided to visit her parents. The Bradley family had not met Lacey, and when Addison spoke to her mother, she said, "Please don't invite my aunts, uncles and cousins because a crowd might overwhelm Lacey. If she stays much longer, we can have a family meal, but I think a small meal would be best for now."

She heard her mother's agreement on the phone. "How long is your current charge staying?"

I'm not sure; the situation feels awkward. Greyson Pellesser, an army officer, was nominated as Lacey's guardian. I doubt Lacey's mother knew about his lifelong commitment to the army, and the challenge of fitting Lacey into his current lifestyle is raising concerns.

"What options are there besides the man? Are there grandparents or other relatives?"

Addison explained about the grandparents and admitted that she had gone onto a database that compared DNA from a person with other samples on their website.

"I might find a relative, although placing her with a stranger is not ideal if someone is willing to take her. Knowing she has cousins or other relatives as she grows might allow her to reach out to them. Also, if there are medical difficulties, having someone with similar DNA might be lifesaving."

The trip to Warburton took about two hours, and halfway through, Addison stopped at a park to use the toilets and let Lacey burn off some energy. Addison was excited to see her parents and eager to get there, but she knew Lacey might feel nervous, so she paused to let her play. When Addison pulled into the driveway, she stopped for a moment, a sense of peace settling over her. This was Addison's childhood home, and although she had bought herself a house in Chessberry, this place would always feel like home. She got out of the car, unbuckled Lacey, and lifted her from the car seat. While Lacey waited beside the car, Addison grabbed their overnight bags and headed to the front door. Before she could knock, the door swung open, and Mrs Bradley wrapped Addison in a warm hug. When they stepped back, Liz Bradley smiled at Lacey.

"Hello, Lacey. I am pleased to meet you. Come inside and meet Addison's dad."

Lacey looked concerned, and Addison knelt next to the little girl.

"You are safe. My dad is not loud, does not issue orders, and does not do anything else that should concern you. Please trust me on this."

Lacey nodded and took Addison's hand.

Tony Bradley rose from his chair and hugged Addison. When they parted, he looked at Lacey and said, "I hope you're looking after my little girl."

Lacey giggled. "Miss Addi isn't little, and she's supposed to look after me."

"Ah, well, we should discuss that over biscuits and Milo. What do you think?"

Lacey took the offered hand, and the shy, awkward child disappeared under her father's careful introduction. Addison smiled at her mother, who shook her head and grinned.

"I'd better find those biscuits if you want to make the Milo, Addi."

The day progressed well, Lacey hanging on every word Tony Bradley addressed to her. Addison and Liz watched with amusement as Tony bewitched the little girl. When Tony suggested a walk around the block, Lacey had her shoes laced up in a flash, and as the two left, the little girl holding the offered hand, Addison sighed. She and her mother sat at the kitchen table with mugs of tea, catching up.

"I thought you said Lacey was shy."

"She fears unknown men and hangs back in groups until someone includes her. The men thing comes from the Major, and the hanging back might be her personality. Or the changes in her life."

"She is delightful. Have you considered adopting her if the soldier can't see his way clear to include her in his life?"

Addison nodded. "Yes, I already am attached to her, and I refuse to allow her to be palmed off on an unknown relative or placed in the foster system. Since we started Facetiming, Greyson seems to be becoming attached to her, so he might change his lifestyle to include her. We'll have to wait and see."

"What is the soldier like?"

"He is an attractive man. It's hard to tell how tall he is since we're FaceTiming while he's sitting in a chair, but he has dark hair cut in the regulation style. Greyson has a square chin and a masculine nose that's not too big, and the most infectious smile. He's lovely with Lacey, kind but jokey. From what the neighbour told me, there was no man in Tammy's life, so once she gets over her fear, Lacey is smitten with the kind men she has met."

Liz Bradley smiled. "And what about you? Are you smitten with the soldier?"

Addison blushed. "I admit I find him attractive, but the idea of anything more than we have with dealing with Lacey is unlikely. He has more than once said that he is in the army for life, so there would be no room for a wife and kids, I'm thinking."

"Oh, well, just keep working with Lacey. She certainly seems different from the girl you described."

Addison nodded. "She had grown so much since I removed her from the Major's care. Lacey even started Guides last week and is having a ball. I offered her sporting options, but she didn't seem keen. I'd like her to learn to swim, but I must choose an instructor carefully. The heated pool in Chessberry makes choosing a time of the year easier, so we'll see how we go."

Over dinner that night, Lacey watched the interaction between Addison and her parents. Finally, she said to Tony, "If you are Miss Addi's dad, can you be my dad, too? I never had one of those."

Tony looked at Addison, and she shook her head slightly. How did they navigate this situation? Tony looked at Lacey and said, "I am Addison's dad, and I can't be your dad, but I could be your grandpa."

Lacey's eyes widened. "Really? You could be my Grandpa? And could Miss Liz be my grandma?"

"She sure could. What do you want to call me? You could stick with Grandpa, Poppy, or Pa. What do you think?"

Lacey giggled at the name Poppy and settled on Pa. After a short discussion, they decided to call Liz Nanna.

Chapter Six

After their trip to Heidelberg, Lacey was excited to tell her classmates she had a grandpa and grandma. Addison had reservations, but decided Lacey could never have too many loving people. Building a network of supportive people was a good move, and knowing that Lacey had previously relied on a kind neighbour supported her thoughts. When Lacey told Grey about her new grandparents, Addison thought she saw disapproval in his expression, but as he celebrated with Lacey, she felt she was mistaken. That night, after Lacey went to bed, Addison was surprised to see Grey's name on her phone read out.

"Hi, Grey. Considering we only spoke a while ago, your call is surprising. What can I do for you?"

"What in damnation are you doing to Lacey? You know I am her guardian and will likely have her living with me. The more connections she makes while staying with you, the harder it will be for her to start a new life with me. Why would you tell her to call your parents Pa and Nana?"

The accusation stung Addison, and she paused for a moment before replying.

"Your premise that a network of safe people for a child is not a good thing shows your total lack of understanding of children in our society. Lacey had only a kindly neighbour to turn to when Tammy died, and now she has multiple people to turn to if she needs help. It interests me that you assume I told Lacey to classify my parents as grandparents, which I did not. She asked my dad if he could be her dad, since he was mine, since she didn't have one of those. We decided it was better to go with the grandparent title. You aren't here, and I know that is not your fault, but I can't run every decision by you; I have to do what I think is best."

There was silence on the phone, and Addison looked at the screen to see if they were disconnected when Grey spoke.

"I know you are doing what you feel is best for Lacey, and considering you're the one with experience, and I have none, I guess I have to bow to your expertise. I'm sorry. I assumed you told Lacey to consider your parents to be grandparents. I wanted to give you a heads-up without Lacey hearing about it. Our time here is nearly over, and the bigwigs are organising our departure. I could be back in a week or two."

"Oh, that's great. Lacey will be so excited, which is good, that she doesn't know more than a day before you arrive; otherwise, she'd drive me mad asking if it was time yet."

"Will you meet me at the base when we arrive? The officers will dismiss us from the parade ground, and it's lonely for the men with nobody to greet them."

"Sure. Give me a time, and I'll make sure we are there."

Greyson cried off his regular chat with Lacey that week, and her disappointment was immense. Addison felt it meant Grey was already preparing to return to Chessberry with his men, but she wouldn't share that thought with Lacey because she didn't want the child to ask her a hundred times a day if Grey was home yet. When Grey's text came, Addison had to admit that she was excited about meeting Grey in person. She organised the day off and chose a sundress for Lacey, explaining that they had an important task to complete and that her school uniform wouldn't be suitable.

Addison's excitement grew as they approached the army base, and Lacey began asking questions. There was a hold-up at the gates as guards checked drivers' identities, and Addison hoped Greyson had included her name on the paperwork. When the guard waved them through without hesitation, Addison sighed with relief and focused on the cadet directing traffic. By now, Lacey was bouncing in her seat, and when Addison released her from her car seat, she said, "Are you ready to see Grey?"

Lacey squealed excitedly, and Addison held her hand to stop her from racing towards the empty parade ground.

The crowd's mood was jubilant, with families and spouses eager to see loved ones they hadn't seen for six months. When the regiment arrived, marching in formation, people cheered, and some cried. Addison had never seen a parade, and the precision of the soldiers stunned her. These individuals had been overseas for months, yet they executed their drills perfectly. With a shouted command, the soldiers halted, and with the order to dismiss, chaos ensued. People ran through the lines of soldiers as they looked for their loved ones. Addison knew she would get lost in the crowd if she left Lacey before they spotted Greyson.

Walking forward tentatively, Addison scanned the lines of soldiers, looking for Grey. Dressed in their uniforms, the men looked alike, and with families gathered around, she despaired of finding Greyson until everyone left. Lacey tugged at her shirt.

"There, Addi, he's there."

When the man lifted his face and smiled, Addison felt her heart lurch, and she released Lacey's hand, allowing the girl to speed through the crowd and throw herself at Greyson. The soldier, who thought he couldn't raise a little girl, scooped her into his arms, and as she hugged him, he returned the cuddle.

Addison walked towards Greyson, seeing him for the first time in person. Her grin at the sight of Lacey and Grey wreathed her face, and she stood by, waiting for the embrace to end. Greyson released Lacey and opened his arms, and Addison laughed and stepped into the embrace. The short hug made her aware of the man's strength. The arms that held her felt firm and muscular, and his chest was equally solid. All the times she had talked to Greyson, she had never realised how well he was built.

As she stepped away, a voice said, "I told you she was beautiful, kind too, because she met your sorry ass today."

Greyson scowled. "Watch the language; there's a child here."

Addison smiled. "I assume you are Striker. Do you have a real name?"

"Welcome me home with a hug, and I'll tell you. This lucky bug, ah, bloke, has two beautiful women, and I have no one."

Despite the bravado of the sentence, Addison could see that the soldier with no one to greet him was sad, so she stepped into his arms and hugged him. Lacey watched the interactions and said, "Should I hug that man, too?"

Addison shook her head. "No one is forcing you to hug anyone, but maybe a thank you because this is the man who set up the video call every time Grey called us."

Lacey smiled shyly and said, "Thank you, Mr Striker."

"You're welcome, sweetheart. And the name is Austin."

Greyson said, "Give me a minute to collect my kitbag, and we can go. Do you want to join us, Striker?"

"Yeah, thanks."

Addison dropped Greyson and Austin at Major Pellesser's house before continuing to their place. Looking at Lacey, Addison thought the little girl's cheeks must ache from smiling, but Lacey's joy gladdened her. After so much that went wrong in the little girl's life, a moment or two of sheer pleasure would help to ease her heart.

When Greyson called an hour later, Addison invited Lacey and her to dinner.

"I thought I should take you two out to dinner."

"Can we take a rain check on that? Lacey is so excited, I doubt she will make it through the meal before she falls asleep. Ask Austin, and I'll ask Cathy, and we'll have an impromptu dinner party. I'm not sure when you usually eat dinner, but Lacey will be asleep before we start if we leave it any later than six o'clock."

After a quick call to Cathy to invite her for dinner, Addison pulled out the casseroles she had prepared that morning and loaded them into the oven. The meal, although simple, would be enough for the four adults if she served them with fresh sourdough bread.

Addison thought about the changes that might occur in their lives now that Greyson was home. Would he visit every day? Would he make arrangements to move Lacey from her home? Addison didn't know the answer to those questions and realised that she and Grey would have to discuss what happened going forward, but for tonight, she intended to enjoy her dinner party.

Cathy arrived before the two men, and after Addison introduced the pair, Austin and Cathy struck up a conversation while Lacey monopolised Grey's attention. Addison watched Grey with Lacey and realised the man was good with the little girl.

"Do you have nephews or nieces, Grey?"

"Yeah, a few of each. I don't see the kids as often as I would like because I always seem to be in a different part of the world from them."

Once she had served the meal, Addison joined in the conversation, and it surprised her to discover that Austin was not resigning when it came time to do so. He said the army had been good to him, but he was ready to return to civilian life.

Addison raised an eyebrow at Grey.

"So, any plans for you to retire, Grey?"

"No, I'm a career man. Once I reach sixty-five, I will retire. Lacey will be my only outside commitment because the army and marriage are incompatible so that I won't go there."

Cathy said, "Don't you miss real life?"

Grey shook his head. "I'm certain Stringer will miss the life once he quits."

Austin shook his head. "I won't miss getting out of bed at the crack of dawn or being told what to do by some old man who should have retired years ago. I won't miss deploying to countries where the locals want to shoot at you, and I won't miss having another three hundred blokes lined up for a meal. I'm ready for my own home, and hopefully, I'll meet a woman who wants to share it with me."

Considering Grey looked angry at the question and Austin's answer, Addison moved the conversation to another topic. Cathy told Grey how well Lacey was doing at school and that while the Major had tried his best, both Lacey and his father were happier with their arrangement with Addison. When Addison noticed Lacey yawning widely, she excused herself to help the little girl put on her pyjamas and settle into bed.

"Can Grey read my story tonight?"

"I'll ask."

Grey looked surprised at the request, and Addison kissed Lacey good night, turned on the night light and left the room.

When she arrived in the kitchen, she found Cathy and Austin clearing the table and stacking the dishwasher.

"Do you want tea or coffee in the lounge room?"

Cathy shook her head. "I'm going to head home, and if I give Austin a ride, you and Grey can discuss where you will go from here."

"Okay. I'll see you tomorrow, Cathy, and I hope to catch up with you again, Austin. You're welcome anytime."

Addison put the kettle on and waited for Grey to finish the story. Sometime later, when he entered the kitchen, Addison grinned.

"What took so long? Did she con you into reading another book?"

Greyson nodded. "I think we're raising a con artist. What happened to Cathy and Austin?"

"They left so we can discuss what happens now."

Greyson nodded. "I have a month's leave, and I thought I would spend as much time with Lacey as possible so she gets used to being with me."

Addison's heart sank. "So you are going to take her with you? You've given up on finding someone else to raise her?"

"Yes. Lacey is an amazing gift Tammy left me, and I want to do the right thing in her memory. I know my decision will come as a surprise because I was against having anything to do with the idea initially, but she is such a nice little girl, I feel compelled to do it."

"Where do you intend to live?"

"Would you rent me a room? I could be on hand often, and if Lacey becomes accustomed to me doing things for her, the transfer from your home to mine will be easier."

Addison considered the request. While the idea was good, the thought of having Grey around all the time made her heart race. The man was a career soldier, and his earlier comment confirmed that he had no plans for marriage, but his presence in her house might give Addison's heart other ideas. Her hesitation caused Greyson to say, "If you find the idea repugnant, I can stay with my father and come over to spend time with Lacey once she finishes school."

"No, no, not repugnant, just unusual. I share my home with random children, but I've never had a man live here. Let's try and see how we go."

Chapter Seven

Greyson moved in the next day, and Addison hoped they could keep their relationship platonic. Lacey was ecstatic that Greyson was living with them, while Addison found herself pushed aside. The two spent time together outside the house, generally only returning to eat and sleep.

Addison thought their togetherness might wane, but it didn't. Left with the washing, ironing, housework and cooking, Addison grew angry. Two weeks after Grey moved in, Addison said, "We need to talk."

Greyson grimaced. "No guy wants to hear those words from a woman's mouth."

Addison placed her hands on her hips. Raising her voice, she said, "And no woman wants to be treated like a damn servant in her own home, doing all the household chores and cooking while her housemates jaunt around the state. If you intend to continue wooing Lacey with me doing all the stuff in the house, then I want you to leave."

After her pronouncement, a stunned silence greeted Addison's tirade.

"Shit. I'm sorry. I got so caught up in trying to have Lacey rely on me that I lost sight of the everyday. I promise we will

pull our weight if you allow me to stay."

A week later, Addison cursed herself for forcing Grey to spend more time in the house. She found his nearness unsettling, and her attraction for the man didn't dim. As she rinsed the plates one night, Grey stood close behind Addison and placed his hands on her hips. With a breathy voice, she said, "What are you doing?"

He turned her and pulled her against him. "I'm going to kiss you unless you tell me no. I've wanted to do this since the day I saw you on the screen, and spending so much time together has made my attraction harder to ignore. So, yes or no?"

"Yes"

Greyson wrapped his fingers in her hair and tilted her head back. The kiss, an exploration at first, turned fiery, and Addison groaned as Grey feasted on her mouth. Sliding her hands beneath his T-shirt, she explored the rugged ridges of his chest and stomach. The exploration made Greyson groan, and his lips worked their way across her neck and shoulders. Pulling away from Addison took more strength than he thought, but he needed to clarify one thing.

"Addi, listen to me. I want you, but our relationship won't lead to marriage. If you accept that, I will love you every night, but I will leave alone when I have to go."

Addison knew that she wanted more, but was it worse to turn him down now and never experience what it was to be with him or sleep with him and suffer grief when he left? Missing out on loving Grey was, to her thought, worse than suffering when he walked away.

"I want whatever you can give me before you have to leave."

Greyson and Addison spent every night together, always mindful that Greyson should move to his bed before Lacey woke. When he had to return to work, Greyson left each morning and returned in time for dinner. Despite being preoccupied with her life, Addison refused to lose contact with her friends, particularly Cathy. Much to her delight, Cathy and Austen seemed like a match made in heaven, and she was sure that Austin had found the woman to share his house when he was finally free.

As the months passed, Greyson began taking Lacey to his flat at the base. The situation wasn't ideal, as there was only one bedroom, but he assured Addison that he had completed the paperwork for a two-bedroom flat. Lacey seemed content to spend the night with Greyson, and Addison realised that the time would come soon when the little girl wouldn't need her. She covered her pain with smiles and encouragement, but each time Lacey chose Greyson over her, it felt like a knife piercing her heart. With Greyson's intention to keep Lacey overnight, Addison and Cathy agreed to have a girls' night on the couch, eating junk food and watching a chick-flick. Before she turned on the television, Cathy said, "Tell me what is happening between you and Greyson. You smile, but you forget I know you better than most, and the smile never reaches your eyes."

"I've set myself up for heartache, and I decided it was better to be with Greyson and miss him than not be with him at all. The problem is that he will leave and take Lacey away from me. I always knew Lacey's time was limited, but after six months or more, it is hard to accept that you were a stopgap, and her real family is now waiting to take over."

"Do you think Greyson will allow you to contact Lacey if they move?"

"I can't see why not, but it might be hard to chat with Lacey, knowing that Greyson is in the background. Enough about me; tell me about you and Austin."

As Cathy gushed about how excellent and considerate Austin was, Addison felt guilty at the jealousy that consumed her. Cathy had everything Addison wanted and was never going to have with Greyson.

Greyson unlocked the door and stepped inside. The sound of vomiting reached him, and he hesitated. When he heard Addison's quiet voice murmuring platitudes to calm his ward, Greyson rushed through the house, where he found the two women in his life together in the bathroom. Lacey leaned over the toilet, her frail body shaking as she vomited again. Addison raised her eyes and said,

"Can you find a cloth to wet and wipe Lacey's face?"

Greyson raced into the kitchen and grabbed a clean cloth from under the sink before returning to the bathroom. Lacey was curled in Addison's lap, weeping quietly. Grey handed the cloth to Addison, and she wiped Lace's sweaty face before rising and heading to her bedroom.

After laying Lacey down on her bed, she said,

"Do you want to stay with her for a minute? I need to get some electrolytes for her and some Panadol."

When Addison returned, she said, "You'd better not get too close. I assume that, as half the school is down with this virus, it spreads quickly. We'd hate to have the defence force out of action."

Addison administered the Panadol and encouraged Lacey to take a few sips of water before tucking the little girl in and motioning for Greyson to leave the room. Addison washed her hands well, but considering her proximity to Lacey, she assumed she would come down with the illness in a day or two. Addison put the kettle on and said, "Hi."

Greyson ran a hand over the scruff, which was beginning to show on his face.

"Holy hell, what was that?"

"There has been a virus sweeping through the school. One day, the kids are fine; the next, they are as sick as dogs. Lacey came down with it yesterday, so I was glad it wasn't a day she was with you, or she could have spread it to you. The bus kids will take the illness with them, but trying to quarantine them is tricky."

Addison looked up when she realised Greyson wasn't speaking, but she was too tired to interpret the angry look on his face. With a shrug, she poured herself a drink and made one for Greyson if he ever stopped leaning against the wall and collected it. Greyson said in a low, controlled voice, "Why didn't you ring me?"

Addison shrugged. "I didn't think of it; I was busy, unless you didn't catch that."

Addison was too tired to argue with Greyson.

"Grey, I was up all night and need to rest now in case Lacey has a relapse. If you want to call in tomorrow to check on her, that would be great. Kids seem to bounce back quickly."

Greyson walked away from the house, his anger growing at how Addison had dismissed him. Didn't she understand that she was the childminder, but he was the guardian?

The following morning, Lacey swore she was well enough to go to school, and against her better judgment, Addison allowed the girl to attend. Determined to check Lacey's status, Addison walked to the classroom Lacey attended to discover that Greyson had collected the child just after morning recess. Addison was furious. Not only had Greyson removed her from school, but he hadn't thought to inform her. With a lunch duty to perform, Addison had no time to follow through on Greyson's behaviour. After his anger last night, Addison knew she needed to clear the air with Grey, as much as she hated the idea, because he would eventually get a two-bedroom flat and move Lacey to the base with him. What would happen to their relationship then? Was he preparing to break up with her? The headache that had plagued Addison for the last hour throbbed, and overthinking hurt. She would put her troubles aside until later.

Tired beyond belief, Addison staggered from the car to the house. She intended to change Lacey's bedding, but a wave of dizziness overwhelmed her and she braced herself against the wall. Knowing she needed supplies beside her bed, she crawled into the kitchen to collect the electrolytes and paracetamol. Lying in bed with the room floating around her, Addison felt awful. When the first wave of nausea hit, Addison lurched up in bed and stumbled towards the toilet.

Wave after wave of nausea hit her, and Addison continued to vomit, even when all she expelled was bile.

Addison lay on the floor sobbing. Her stomach ached, and while she had emptied her stomach with her earlier purges, she continued to dry heave. Trying to move only made her dizziness worse, but Addison knew she needed help. Dragging herself, she reached for her bag lying on her bed and pulled out her phone. The first number she tried was Cathy's, but her phone went to voicemail. She vaguely remembered Cathy talking about visiting her parents, so she dialled Greyson's phone. When his phone went to the message bank, she said, "Grey, please, I need help. Answer me, please."

When he didn't call back, Addison lay her head against the cool tile before dialling her parents' number.

"Hi, darl, this is a nice surprise."

Tony Bradley cut off his conversation when he heard Addison's sobs.

"Dad, I need help. Can you please come?"

Exhausted, Addison lay on the floor, waiting for help to arrive. Before she passed out, it occurred to her that she needed to broaden her social circle.

Chapter Eight

Earlier, when Greyson rang Addison to check on Lacey, the call went unanswered, and he wondered why. Addison silenced her phone if she was in class, but surely she hadn't left Lacey alone. Suddenly, a thought struck him, and he dialled the school, only to discover that Lacey was in class. Greyson was furious, but he kept his voice under control and informed the receptionist that, after her illness yesterday, Lacey should be resting today and that he would collect her shortly. Grey knew he was being a prat for not notifying Addison, but he was too angry to be civil now. He let himself into Addison's house and packed a bag for Lacey before he returned to the base.

The next day, Lacey rode the bus to school, and it was late by the time Greyson collected her from the after-school care centre at the base. He was angry that Addison hadn't called him about Lacey's condition, but he knew that his current anger at her for allowing Lacey to attend school would only lead to an argument if he called her. After they arrived home, Grey told Lacey of his plans for the weekend. Lacey said that Addison was absent, but he waved away her concerns. He planned a trip to a theme park four hours away and decided that he and Lacey could stay overnight and visit a second theme park before returning home Sunday afternoon.

Lacey got bored in the car on their drive to the theme park and asked, "*Are we there yet?*" numerous times. Once they arrived, Lacey was excited as she took in the sights. They visited the displays, and Grey picked the more sedate rides for Lacey to try, though she protested that she couldn't try some of the more adventurous ones. Grey promised they would return when she was bigger, and she could try the rides then. The weekend passed in a blur of rides, displays and junk food, and Grey was as tired as Lacey when they arrived back at the base.

The next morning, Lacey was hard to rouse, but Grey got her organised before the bus arrived. As he kissed Lacey goodbye, he frowned.

"What have you got there?"

"It's a book with pictures of some of the rides I went on. I want to show it to Miss Addi."

"Oh, okay. Don't lose it, though, or the next time we go, you won't remember the rides you want to try."

Once Greyson arrived at work, an email from the housing department notified him that a two-bedroom unit was becoming available and that he should contact the department directly if he were still interested. After completing the paperwork, Greyson returned to his desk and knew he would have to shelve his anger and face Addison. He knew she would be sad that he was removing Lacey from her house, though he had been doing so with increasing frequency recently. When he gave himself time to think, he missed her and knew that Addison would leave a big hole in his life when he moved on. Occasionally, he wondered if they could have a future, but shoved those thoughts aside. Greyson had seen how difficult life was for his mother, raising three rowdy boys without a male role model. How could he do that to another woman, particularly one he cared for? Even as he shoved the idea of marriage into the corner of his mind, images of Striker and Cathy together flittered through his mind.

When Grayson collected Lacey from the care centre, she looked sad.

"What's up, Lacey? Did something happen at school?"

"Miss Addi wasn't at school, and Miss Davenport said she was sick."

"Ah, she must have caught your bug. I'm sure she will be back at school tomorrow."

"Can we go and see her?"

"That's not a good idea if she is sick because we don't want you to get the bug again."

The following day, memories of Lacey's illness and Addison's care for the child, even though she knew she was placing herself in danger of being infected too, plagued Greyson. He rang the school and asked to speak to Addison, but the receptionist told him she was on sick leave. By the end of the day, he was concerned about Addison's welfare and decided to let the care centre know he would be late, then headed towards Addison's house. Should he buy flowers? The romantic gesture seemed wrong if she was still too ill to appreciate it. A car in her driveway gave him second thoughts, but he was here now, so he would check on her and then leave.

He still had his key, but letting himself into the house with visitors present didn't seem right. When the door opened, Greyson found himself face-to-face with Tony Bradley. He grinned and held out his hand, but Addison's dad stared at him and didn't take the offered hand.

"Nice of you to finally arrive. I guess you've been too busy with important things to check on Addison."

"Tony, let the man in. We don't want the neighbours to know our business."

Greyson entered the place that always felt like home and turned to face Tony.

"I came to check on Addison, but it seems I've missed something."

"You sure have. Check your phone. Did Addi try calling you on Friday?"

Greyson flicked through his phone and came across Addison's call on Friday. He remembered that when he saw it, he was still angry and let the call go to voicemail. Addi had left a message that he didn't bother listening to.

"Yes, she did. It went to the message bank, but I was busy and didn't return her call. Why is that important?"

Liz touched Ton's arm and quietly said, "It was important because she was reaching out for help. She couldn't get Cathy because she was away, and couldn't get you because you refused to pick up, so she rang us. Our girl lay on the cold floor, unconscious, for ninety minutes as Tony broke every speed limit in the book to get here."

Greyson's face paled, and he staggered. The knowledge that he had deliberately avoided Addison's call made him feel ill.

"Is she... is she.. alright?"

Tony said, "Yeah, no thanks to you. When we arrived, Liz called an ambulance, and she has been in the hospital since."

Liz said, "She was dehydrated, and her electrolyte levels were too low. The doctors were concerned about kidney failure. She has been on a drip for the past four days and is due to be released tomorrow. She has the remainder of the week off."

"Damn, I'm sorry. We argued about Lacey, and I was angry, so I avoided the call. I can't believe she was so sick, and I ignored her."

"If you had shown her the courtesy of listening to her call," Tony Bradley said, "argument or not, we might have avoided the hospital stay. I don't know if Addison will want to see you when the doctors release her from the hospital; that will be her call. But I don't want you to show your face again until we leave."

Grey couldn't believe he had ruined his friendship with these people and placed Addison in danger. Lacey's guardianship changed his life and his focus; while the army was still vital, he realised that doing the right thing by Lacey consumed his life. Grey's anger at Addison for keeping Lacey's illness from him and sending her to school when she should have been recovering blinded him to other facts. How could he not have remembered that Addison had taken Lacey in when she was alone, and that, before he returned from overseas, the two had a strong bond? Addison had never placed her desires before the care of the little girl, and after treating her illness, it was apparent that she might suffer some sickness as a result. How could he have ignored Addison's health and spent the weekend at theme parks instead of caring for her? Removing Lacey from school without talking to Addison was wrong, and he regretted his anger and poor behaviour. Would Addison ever forgive him? That was something he wouldn't know until her parents left.

Unable to visit Addison, Grey spent his time out of work preparing the new accommodation. The place was clean and well-appointed, but Grey wanted to buy a bed for Lacey and girly-type linen for her bedroom. He could have used some help, but since he couldn't contact Addison, Grey called Striker instead.

"Hey mate, can you give me Cathy's mobile number? I need help preparing Lacey's new bedroom and girly stuff, and I don't mix."

"I'm not sure Cathy is speaking to you. She feels bad that we went away, but you didn't plan your trip until you left work on Friday. If you had checked up on Addison, she mightn't have had to go to the hospital."

Greyson sighed. "I regret what I did, but it never occurred to me she would be so sick. Considering what I did, I feel like a jerk, but I can't see her until her parents leave, so I thought I'd pretty up the new flat."

"I'll give you the number, but don't be surprised if she is rude."

Despite her anger at Greyson's behaviour, Cathy agreed to help him with the girly bedding and linen he wanted to buy for Lacey. Before they headed for the shops, Greyson expressed his remorse and desire to see Addison and apologise for his neglect.

Chapter Nine

The new flat and the girly linens were a big hit with Lacey, and Grey felt grateful that he had done something right. When Lacey arrived home from school with a beaming smile, he asked her about it.

"Miss Addi was at school today. She said she went to the hospital but is all better now."

"That's great. Maybe we can visit tomorrow after work."

The following day, Greyson rang Addison. When Addison saw the readout on the phone, she almost left it to voicemail, but if she pushed too hard, she would rarely see Lacey anywhere but at school. According to Cathy, he had moved into a two-bedroom flat and asked her to help him with girly things for Lacey's room. She wondered why he hadn't asked her, but she guessed her father's disgust may have had something to do with it.

"Hello, Greyson. What can I do for you?"

"I wanted to say how sorry I am for what happened to you, and hoped Lacey and I could come and visit."

"I would love to see Lacey somewhere other than school, so yes, you can visit. Do you want to come for dinner?"

After they organised a night for the visit, Greyson ended the call. He knew that Addison wanted to see Lacey and had left unsaid that she didn't want to see him. Even if he had to use Lacey as a tool, he wanted to get back in Addison's good books.

The next day, during their lunch break, Addison told Cathy that Greyson and Lacey were coming for dinner.

"Addi, are you sure that's a good idea? Maybe you can't blame Greyson for skipping out on you, but since he moved Lacey to the barracks, you struggle to see her. Having them back in the house will make it harder to let Lacey go when he gets a transfer."

"I know, I know, but I miss her so much, and knowing that she lives so close and I can't see her every day, I want to take this opportunity before they move somewhere else."

When the doorbell rang, Addison took a deep breath. She hadn't seen Greyson since their argument about Lacey's illness, so things were bound to be awkward. Opening the door was like taking a cork from a shaken bottle; Lacey launched herself at Addison and hugged her tightly. Addison hugged the child, realising she missed this interaction with the girl. Greyson stood in the doorway watching the reunion and felt bad about keeping them apart, although it wasn't intentional.

"Greyson, come in. If you want to grab a coffee, Lacey can help me prepare dinner."

While Lacey and Addison chatted as they made dinner, Greyson wanted to be part of the conversation instead of a bystander. Dinner was a simple casserole, and over the meal, they chatted as Lacey told Addison about her fabulous new bedroom. Greyson was thankful that Addison directed some comments to him, so although they weren't wholly comfortable, Greyson hoped that they would come to an agreement with each other.

Once they finished the meal, Greyson set Lacey up in front of the television and returned to help Addison with the dishes.

"You don't need to help; I can do these when you go."

Greyson raised an eyebrow. "Are you that eager to get rid of me?"

Addison blushed and said, "I didn't think you would want to stay."

"Addi, we need to talk, so if helping you with the dishes helps, then that's what I'll do."

Addison placed the last dish in the dishwasher and sat at the table.

"Okay, say what you have to say."

"First, can I say how damned sorry I am that I didn't answer your call? I let it go to the message bank and refused to listen to your message because I was still angry with you. After your father told me what a worthless human being I was, I reviewed my actions and realised that where Lacey is concerned, I have become hyper-sensitive and controlling. I didn't acknowledge that you were busy caring for Lacey and didn't have time to hold my hand; I just got offended and angry. Can you answer a question for me? Why did you send Lacey to school on Thursday?"

"It was against my better judgment, but Lacey insisted she was fine and would come and find me if she felt unwell or too tired. Imagine my shock when I checked on her, and she was gone."

"I realised it was a dick move, taking her without letting you know, but I was angry that you were so concerned about your job that you took her to school after she had been so unwell. It didn't occur to me that she might have wanted to go."

"So, where do you want to go from here?"

"Can we return to having a meal together once a week like saw used to? I know you want to see Lacey out of school, and I miss your company. We might never return to our easy relationship, but I'd like to repair our friendship."

"Okay, I'd like that, but now and then, you have to buy takeout so that I am not always the cook."

Greyson grinned. "I can do that. Now, it must be time for me to take Lacey home, but I'll talk to you soon."

As Greyson and Lacey drove away, Addison wondered if her agreement with Greyson would lead to more heartache. She knew that Cathy would think she was foolish for entertaining Greyson's idea, and Addison knew that when he packed his bags and relocated, she would be heartbroken. Still, Addison convinced herself that something was better than nothing.

The weekly meal was when Addison and Lacey could reconnect, and Addison had to admit that it was nice having Greyson in the house. They kept their relationship strictly platonic, though Addison sometimes caught Greyson looking at her, and what she saw in his eyes was desire. The attraction she had felt for him the first time she saw him on the screen had never diminished, but she knew a more intimate relationship would leave her gutted when he left.

A month after their first meal, Lacey entered the house with a grin and holding a bag.

"What are you grinning about, madam?"

"Grey and I are having a sleepover with you. I have my pyjamas and uniform for tomorrow, and Grey says he will go to the flat to change in the morning."

Addison's eyes widened, and Greyson said, "Is that okay?"

How did she tell the excited child that her guardian had overstepped the mark and it was not okay?

"Oh, sure. Why don't you put your things in your room?"

When Lacey left the room, Addison swung around to face Greyson. "What the hell?"

"Lacey asked, but I didn't have the heart to refuse. I can use the bedroom I rented for that first month, and we can all have breakfast together."

Two weeks later, Addison extracted herself from the arms that held her pressed up against his chest and wondered at her sanity.

"Grey, wake up. You have to move bedrooms."

The sexy soldier currently occupying her bed groaned.

"Can't I stay here for a while? Lacey won't be awake yet."

"No, because we will go back to sleep, and she'll catch us."

Grey hauled himself from the bed. "We need to talk about what happened last night."

Addison screwed up her face. "I don't think a broken condom at this stage of my cycle will be any problem."

Greyson sighed. "If it is, let me know."

As Addison prepared breakfast, she prayed that the comment she made about the broken condom was valid. Who knew when conception could occur? Even religious groups that banned contraception other than the rhythm method got it wrong. She would keep her fingers crossed that the contraception failure didn't result in a pregnancy. Pushing the problem to the back of her mind, Addison wanted to enjoy every moment of Grey's presence because she would miss him terribly when he moved to another state, which she feared was inevitable.

Addison's phone rang as she drove towards home. Despite her desire to answer the device, Addison knew the dangers of being distracted, and if she answered it, she feared that a police car would drive past. Whoever was calling could leave a message or ring back. The phone rang again as she unpacked the car and carted the groceries to the house. Lowering the bags onto the kitchen counter, Addison answered the phone.

"God, Addi, I've been trying to reach you for ages."

"I did some shopping after work, so sue me."

"I know tonight isn't the night we come for dinner, but I need to see you without Lacey. Can I come tonight?"

"Sure. Do you want a meal?"

"No thanks, just a chat."

Before Greyson arrived, Addison showered and changed, and while his tone wasn't suggestive or flirtatious, she decided to wear jeans and a shirt instead of her usual sweats. When she heard the car in the driveway, she opened the front door and watched as Greyson approached her. Although she couldn't pinpoint the problem, something bothered Grey; his body was stiff, and his face serious. He kissed her cheek and said, "Can we talk?"

Addison stepped aside so he could enter, and she followed him as he headed for the kitchen. Greyson leaned against the bench and said, "I have something to tell you that will be unwelcome. About six months ago. Before you and I became involved, I applied for a promotion. The promotion came with a transfer, and today, personnel notified me that I was successful. Lacey and I are transferring to the Kyana base in a week. I have to report for duty on Monday next week."

Addison's mouth fell open, and then she slumped into a chair. As tears welled in her eyes, Greyson ran his hand through his hair, sighed and said, "I always told you I wouldn't marry you. Surely it occurred to you that I would get a transfer someday?"

"Just because it was a possibility didn't mean it was imminent. When are you leaving?"

"I've been granted a week off and hope to wind up my affairs here by Friday. We will leave first thing Saturday morning. I have to enrol Lacey at a new school next week and organise childcare. I hope they have Guides in their community because she enjoys that, but the swimming pool is not heated, so she won't be able to swim until it gets warmer."

"Thanks for telling me before I heard it on the grapevine. What does Lacey think about the move?"

"She's apprehensive, but I've convinced her it will be an adventure."

Greyson absent-mindedly kissed Addison on the cheek as he left, his mind already on the logistics of the move. When he backed his car out of her driveway, Addison let the tears fall. How was it that she had everything she wanted, and with one flick of a pen, it was all gone?

Chapter Ten

Addison held Lacey tightly, tears streaming down her face. Who would've thought that when she took in a frightened girl, she would blossom into the bright, happy child she is now? Saying farewell to foster kids was almost routine, as Addison only provided emergency accommodation. Still, Lacey wasn't the usual client, and since the child had touched her heart, this goodbye was much harder.

"Lacey, we have to go."

Addison glanced up at Greyson and knew that he felt sympathy for her. As Grey took Lacey's hand, he pulled Addison against himself with his other hand and kissed her. The kiss was not filled with heat and passion, but was a loving goodbye.

Once Grayson and Lacey drove away, Addison made herself a cup of tea, laced it with brandy and curled up on the couch. She didn't know how long she had slept, but the banging on the door roused her. Cathy and Austin stood at the door, and the sight of her best friend caused another attack of weeping. With Cathy's arms around her, all of Addison's pent-up grief welled out. When Addison's tears finally dried, she said, "Give me a minute to clean up; I must look a mess."

After Addison washed her face, she returned to the kitchen to discover that Cathy had made drinks and Austin was plating doughnuts and other pastries. Once she sat, Addison looked at her friends.

"You guys are the best. Thanks for this; I needed a distraction. Letting a foster child go is always challenging, but Lacey was more than that, and to have Grey walk away without a backward glance is soul-destroying. Even with phone calls and FaceTime calls, I will lose so much of Lacey's life that the burden of keeping in touch will eventually be too much, and we will lose contact altogether."

Cathy asked, "Did Grey say he would contact you?"

"No, his mantra about being in the army for a lifetime excuses him from continuing our connection. I hope when he is old and lonely, he looks back on what he could have had and regrets his choices."

Austin shook his head and sighed. "I think his father's lack of engagement when he was a child affected Grey strongly. The question I asked, and he could never answer, was if the armed forces impacted his childhood, why did he join?"

Cathy nodded. "Surely he can see how his father's life turned out? The man can't hold a civil conversation without giving orders, and he has been alone since his wife died."

"Grey said he wasn't the marrying kind when we got together, but he's accepted being Lacey's guardian so well that I hoped he might change his mind."

"Addi, maybe it is time to remove your name from the foster emergency list. You've had a couple of tough gigs with Tyler and then Lacey, and I fear for your well-being if you continue to have to say goodbye to these kids that wriggle their way into your heart."

Addison nodded. "I know what you're saying, Cathy, but so many kids need help. I might tell Stella I'm taking a break to give my heart time to heal."

The following weeks dragged for Addison, and although Grey never said he'd contact her, she ached to hear his voice and talk to Lacey. Did Lacey like her new school? Had she made friends? Who was her sitter when Grey was at work? Addison had so many questions she longed to ask, but she wouldn't have answers unless she made contact. The thought of calling Greyson made Addison nervous, so she poured a glass of wine, loaded her favourite playlist for background noise, and dialled his number. Timing the call so that Lacey would be in bed, Addison hoped Grey would organise some calls between her and Lacey.

"Addison, why are you calling?"

"Uh… Hello to you, too. I'm calling to find out how you're settling in and hopefully schedule a time for Lacey and me to talk."

There was a moment-long pause, and Addison checked her phone to see if she had lost contact with Greyson. When he spoke, the tone told Addison that whatever came next would not make her happy.

"Addison, I don't think calling would be a good idea. Lacey has made school friends and adapted far better than I thought she would. I'm sorry, but talking to you will unsettle her so that I won't allow calls."

Addison's breath caught in her throat. "Please, Grey, I won't upset her, but I miss her and want to talk to her."

"No. And Addison, we had an affair, and it always had an expiration date, which has passed. I don't want to be cruel, but please don't call again."

When Grey hung up, Addison was left listening to silence. The ache in her heart would take years to dull, and if she ever heard from Lacey again, it might be when she turned eighteen. Would Addison ever know if Lacey married and had children or chose a high-profile job that made her rich? She finally understood that Greyson had thought of her as nothing more than a babysitter and a convenient lover, neither of which he valued highly.

Addison spent the weekend cleaning and purging her home of anything that reminded her of Lacey or Greyson. She packed away the drawings, fridge magnets, hair ties and clips from the bathroom. Bubble bath, baby shampoo and talc ended up in the rubbish bin. The mug that Lacey gave her for her birthday joined the objects in the box, and after a quick check through the washing basket, she retrieved a pair of frilly socks and a T-shirt. Addison replaced the girly doona cover with a generic patterned cover and, with regret, placed the doona cover that Lacey loved in the box and sealed it. Ridding her house of traces of Greyson was easy; it appeared he had removed all evidence of his presence when he packed his bag. Hopefully, without constant reminders of what she had lost, the healing process might be more manageable.

As she threw herself into her work, Addison frequently arrived home around dinner time, and cooking for one had no appeal, so takeout and frozen dinners became the norm. She constantly felt tired and became irritable, snapping at children and other staff. When the phone rang, Addison was almost afraid to answer. Would this be another child in need? Addison didn't think she could handle a troubled child in her present mindset.

"Hi, honey. How are you?"

"Hi, mum. I nearly didn't answer, fearing it would be Stella begging me to take a child."

"Hmm, why would that cause you concern?"

"I am so tired I can hardly get out of my own way. I've been snapping at the kids, and while I know I'm doing it, I can't stop."

"Well, that makes my invitation well-timed. You have three days off, and I bet you are tired from working hard to forget your empty home. Come home, Addi. It might be the tonic that helps you move on."

Addison was on the road within half an hour of her mother's call. Winding down the window and turning up the music helped ease the fatigue. After a short toilet stop at a service station that marked the halfway mark, Addison drove on. When she pulled into the driveway and walked into her mother's hug, she wondered why she had left this trip for so long. Setting her aside to look at her daughter, Liz could see Addison's face, but her mother didn't comment on the pale skin and the black smudges under her daughter's eyes. Liz Bradley thought her daughter had lost weight, so she decided to feed her this weekend. Tony Bradley wasn't as diplomatic as his wife.

"Good grief, Addi, what have you done to yourself? You look as pale as a ghost, and you could pack lunch in the bags under your eyes.

Unless you've started a new trend of buying clothes that are too big, you must have lost kilos. What gives, sweetheart?"

Addi could withstand her mother's scrutiny, but she dissolved into tears when her father, who rarely noticed changes in appearance, commented on how she looked. After hugging her, Tony Bradley said, "I'll get your bags, and you need to sit in the kitchen while your mum makes you a drink. Over dinner, we need to get to the bottom of what is happening."

The conversation at dinner time was painful, but Addison wanted her parents to understand exactly what had happened between her and Greyson. The refusal to let Addison speak to the little girl angered her parents, but they could do nothing about Greyson's callous disregard for Addison's feelings. Although she knew she needed to eat, Addison had little appetite. Liz made all of Addison's favourite foods, but they didn't appeal to Addison. Scrutinising her daughter, Liz said, "Addison, could you be pregnant?"Addison opened her mouth to deny the question when the broken condom episode flashed into her mind.

"Oh, my God."

"I'll take that as a positive. Let me give you a cuppa, and then I'll head to the pharmacy to buy a couple of tests."

Addison looked at the red lines and groaned. She collected the positive test results and brought them out to show her mother.

"Oh, dear. We probably need some time to let this sink in, and then we must make some plans. Do you think Greyson will be supportive?"

Addison shook her head. "When we knew there was a possibility of a pregnancy, he said we'd sort it out together, but his attitude to me has changed so much that I doubt he'd put his hand up to support me."

Liz and Addison discussed options until Addison said, "I have no moral objection to women terminating pregnancies, but it's not the right thing for me."

Tony Bradley was not amused when he heard Addison's news, and he was all for calling Greyson and telling him to man up, but Addison knew she would have to be the one to break the news to Grey.

"Well, that explains the fatigue and disinterest in food. Do you want to see Doc Allen, or do you want to visit someone on Chessberry? If you see Doc Allen, your mum could go with you."

Addison was glad that he dad wasn't criticising her for being careless and was offering suggestions. Eventually, Addison decided to see her doctor in Chessberry because the baby would be born there, so she might as well organise her long term plans.

Before she left her parents' place, Addison phoned her doctor to make an appointment. The appointment was outside school hours because Addison wanted Cathy to be her support person, and they couldn't miss school on the same day. When Addison told Cathy the news, she saw the look that had passed between her friend and Austin.

"What was that look?"

Austin said, "Cathy told me weeks ago she thought you were pregnant."

Addison glared at Cathy. "Could you not have shared that with me? I've been exhausted, suffering with fatigue every night, and eating seems to be off the table, but a heads-up would have been good."

Cathy shrugged. "I thought about telling you, but you seemed to have so much on your plate, I didn't want to add to your woes."

Austin smiled and said, "Congratulations. Will you go through the pregnancy, and will you tell Grey?"

Addison frowned. "Yes, I'm going to have the baby, but telling Grey will be hard because I doubt he will be happy. I'll wait until after the doctor's appointment when they confirm the pregnancy, and then I'll try to contact him."

Chapter Eleven

With the pregnancy confirmed, Addison knew she had to tell Grey about what had happened. After making a cup of camomile tea, Addison dialled Greyson's number. She frowned when her call went straight to the message bank, but she left a message telling Gretson she needed to talk to him. On the third day, Addison tried the phone again, but there was still no response; the system didn't ring. Had he blocked her? What should she do? Addison fired up her computer and looked for the emails she and Greyson had sent when he was still overseas. Without giving him a reason for her request, Addison sent the message.

The following day after school, Addison sat on the couch with her PC in her lap, scrolling through her emails, hoping for a response from Greyson. She looked at the address of the message she'd sent to Greyson, which now showed a notice that the system couldn't deliver it. So, he blocked her on all social media because weeks ago, she tried to access his Facebook page to see if there were photos of Lacey. His account was private, and Grey denied her friend's request. She was unsure if she felt more angry or more devastated by Greyson's actions.

"Cathy, hi. I have a problem. Is Austin at your house? I have to ask him something. Can I come over?"

When Addison arrived at Cathy's place, her friend greeted her and said, "Come into the kitchen. While you talk to Austin, I'll fill you up on doughnuts."

"I know I have to eat, but putting the baby into a sugar coma is not what the doctor ordered."

"I know that, but once won't hurt."

Austin walked into the kitchen, kissed Cathy and then focused on Addison.

"What can I help you with?"

"I have been trying to tell Greyson about the baby, but he has refused my friend request on Facebook and blocked my phone number and emails. I guess the messages are going to the junk mail folder. I hoped you might call and tell him he should ring me."

Austin shook his head. "Grey and I never swapped numbers, but I could try the number you have."

After numerous attempts, it became clear that Grey had changed his mobile number. "What do I do now? I could write a letter, but there is no guarantee he would read it. I doubt that he will be happy, and he should know about his child before it turns eighteen and goes looking for him."

Austin said, "I have a suggestion that might get a response. Call the garrison and ask the personnel to pass on a message."

"Okay, I'll do that now."

Addison hunted for a number from her Google account, and her nerves made it hard to speak when she dialled. Clearing her throat, she said, "I have a message for

Lieutenant Greyson Pellesser. My name is Addison Bradley, and I must contact him."

"Yes, certainly, maám. I will see that the lieutenant gets the message."

A week later, Cathy collected Addison, and the women went to the newly opened vegetarian restaurant. Addison shook her head and said, "When did you go vegetarian?"

"When I realised that you avoid eating anything that contains meat. I've noticed your face turns green whenever someone sits down and eats a burger at work, so I thought I'd offer a solution. Let's see if we can get some food into you."

Addison realised that Cathy was right, and the two women scanned the menu. They chatted until the waitress set their meals before them, and for the first time in weeks, Addison ate with gusto.

"Gosh, Cathy, this is so good. You are brilliant."

"I am brilliant, but I'm also nosy. Did Greyson respond to the message that I'm sure he received?"

"No."

"Do you care if he gets angry? Because I have a brilliant idea that will get a response, but it might be a shouty, angry response."

"Honestly, any response would be an improvement on nothing."

As Cathy told Addison her suggestion for eliciting a response from Greyson, she laughed.

"We can't do that here, but I will do that tomorrow after work. Do you want to come over while I make the call and hang around to see if I get a response? Ask Austin, and I will order something vegetarian. You'd better warn him before he accepts."

The next evening, with Cathy and Austin sitting with her in the lounge room, Addison dialled the number she had used a week ago. A peppy young man answered the phone, and Addison took a breath.

"Good evening. My name is Addison Bradley, and I rang a week ago to leave a message for Lieutenant Pellesser to contact me. He has failed to do so."

"Ah, ma'am, not to be disrespectful, but the lieu said you were stalking him, and we shouldn't pass on any more messages."

"I understand that instruction places you in an awkward position, so you might want to okay my message with your commander or someone else in authority. Please tell Greyson that I am pregnant, and my stalking, as he calls it, has been me attempting to inform him of my condition. I hope your superiors see their way clear to passing on my message. Thank you."

There was a moment's silence when she hung up, and as Cathy laughed, Austin slow-clapped her.

"God, Addi, that was masterful. Now, everyone in the whole damn place will know you are pregnant, and he will have to answer to the commander as to why he has blocked you. I suspect you will get a phone call before the night is out."

Cathy dished as Addi made drinks for them all, and as she sat to eat, Addi felt blessed to have good friends. They had finished dinner and were busy cleaning up when the phone rang. Austin and Cathy grinned, but Addison had to admit that she feared what Greyson would say.

"Come into the lounge room, and I will put it on speaker so you can hear too."

"Hello, this is Addison."

"Damnation, Addison, you made me the talk of the base. The commander bawled me out about my obligations, and I felt like a fool. Why the hell did you have to tell the whole damn base?"

"I told the whole damn base because you refused my friend request on Facebook, you blocked my phone number, and you marked my emails to go to junk mail. I considered writing you a letter, but figured you'd throw it away unread. Being out of contact with everyone means if something happens to your father or brothers, you'll hear about it months after the event, if ever."

"Whatever. The baby, I guess it is mine?"

Stunned silence greeted the question.

Addison blinked back tears and said, "I'm not sure. I could be the mailman's baby, and there was a sexy guy at the pub one night that I hooked up with. If the baby is born with slanty eyes or is black, we'll know it's not yours. Until then, I'll work on the assumption that you are the father."

Austin said, "Greyson Pellesser, you are a piece of work. How could you even ask that question?"

" Jesus, Addi, you said you thought we were safe, and now you tell me you're pregnant. I can't deal with the complications of another child. I suggest you terminate the pregnancy. I don't want to be tied down for the next eighteen years, paying child support. I don't know what a termination costs, but I can send money to cover that if you like."

Addison gasped at the callous way Greyson spoke about the pregnancy."I don't want your money, and I will take care of the pregnancy myself. You are in the clear. You may have blocked me, but you are dead to me after this conversation. Goodbye."

Addison looked at her friends and burst into tears. How had she ever thought Grey was a decent man? When she calmed herself, Cathy asked, "What will you do?"

"Greyson's attitude and suggestion have no bearing on my decision about having the baby. To save him a lifetime of pain, I will fill in the section of the birth certificate where it asks for the father with unknown."

"Cathy, will you be my support person? If I book appointments outside school hours, will you come with me?"

"Yes, I will, but have you told your parents? Your mother might want to help."

Addison laughed. "No woman wants her mother to hear her shouting insults and screaming in agony. No, I'll tell my parents, but having Mum in the birth suite is not an option."

"Gosh, Addison, maybe I'm not up to the job if that happens."

Austin laughed. "You will be fine, and if you run out of the birthing suite, I will have to take your place, and I'm sure no one wants me looking at Addi's privates as she births a baby."

After a stunned silence, Addison began to laugh, and Cathy joined in. "The thought of your horrified face, darl, is enough to make me brave and stay by Addi's side."

Austin sighed. "Thank god."

Chapter Twelve

Although Addison had little to do with the Major since she had relieved him of Lacey's care, the man called in to check on her each week now that she carried his grandbaby. Addison asked the man to share a meal over the weekend, and this invitation became a standing one. A month or two after they began their visits, the Major, who told Addison to call him James, discussed Lacey's mother.

"You know, Beryl tried to find the girl when it became known that her parents had disowned her, but without luck. I admit I wasn't around much, but with three boisterous sons, Beryl loved Tammy like a daughter. It broke her heart that she couldn't find the girl, and it would devastate her to know that the authorities buried her in a pauper's grave."

Addison shook her head. "I didn't know that still happened. I know that it happened in the olden days, but it seems heartless in this day and age."

"The issue has been plaguing me for a while, and I want to find where they buried Tammy and move her to the plot next to Beryl. The woman who packed Lacey's belongings would she know the whereabouts of Tammy's grave?"

"If anyone does, it would be Mrs Francis. There would be a lot of paperwork involved in exhuming a body and relocating it."

The Major shrugged. "If there is one thing I have at the moment is time. Do you know how to contact the woman?"

"We'd have to go for a drive. The last time I asked about a phone number, Mrs Francis said there was little point in spending money on a phone when nobody rang her. I gave her my number and told her to call if she needed help, but I doubted she would."

"Are you up for a drive?"

James Pellesser and Addison drove to Heidelberg the following weekend to visit Mrs Francis. The woman was happy to receive visitors, and when James explained the reason for their visit, Mrs Francis teared up.

"It broke my heart to have her buried with homeless people and other unfortunates, but I didn't have the money to fund her funeral. I imagine there are various forms and paperwork to exhume and relocate a body."

James nodded. "Addison already warned me of that fact, but I feel like it is the right thing to do. My late wife wanted to find Tammy when her parents disowned her, but she failed. I don't intend to fail on seeing the girl buried decently, and a plot beside my wife will help set the matter right."

After much discussion, James agreed to return later in the week and would remain with Mrs Francis until the relocation of Tammy's body was complete. As they drove home, Addison said, "You realise that Mrs Francis is financially stretched and feeding you will place a strain on her?"

James nodded. "I may be out of touch with the real world, but it was obvious that the woman was only just making ends meet. I intend to pay my way and more, so don't fret."

For the remainder of the journey, Addison and James chatted, and when he dropped her off at home, she wished him well on the challenge ahead of him.

"Keep me updated, and if you have a short ceremony when you have her interned beside your wife, I would like to attend."

James smiled, a most unusual expression for the dour man.

"I will let you know."

As she approached her fourth month, Addison stopped feeling constantly nauseous, but fatigue hit her at the end of each day. Her nightly routine had become set, and she either made a meal so she could reheat the leftovers the following day or ordered take-out from the vegetarian restaurant that had become her favourite. Addison was tucked up in bed with a book when the phone rang, startling her.

Reaching over to her nightstand, she answered the call with trepidation. From her experience, calls that came at night generally signalled a child in trouble, but she hoped she was wrong in her assumption. A whispering voice said, "Addi, can you come and get me? I'm scared Mum's boyfriend is going to hurt me."

"Tye?"

"Yes."

"Okay, but first, close your bedroom door and shove your thongs in the gap at the bottom. That will stop the man from entering your bedroom. Can you do that?"

"Yes."

"Good, do it now while I wait."

A minute later, Tyler said, "I've done it. Now what?"

"Pack a few things in your school bag and climb out the window. Hide in the shadows. I will ring the police to pick you up and keep you safe until I arrive. What's the address there?"

She heard the fear in Tyler's voice. "502 Burns Street, Macedon."

"Okay, get organised and get out. I'll see you soon, but the police will contact you first. Okay?"

"Okay."

Addison hated hanging up, but she knew she had to get the local cops on board for this to work. She was about two hours away from Macedon and couldn't allow Tyler to hide in the streets for two hours. Addison dressed in jeans and a t-shirt, struggling into her clothes as she searched for the number of the police station. A tired voice answered, and Addison said, "My name is Addison Bradley, and I have a serious foster situation that I will need your assistance with. Are you the right person to speak with, or is there someone more senior to discuss my problem?"

"If you hold a minute, I will put you through to the Sergeant."

Addison explained her problem to the receptive man at the end of the phone. "So you want me to pick him up?"

"Yes, he is currently hiding in the shadows in the street. I don't want to tell you your job, but if you park a house or two away from the address and flick your lights a couple of times, Tyler will find you."

"And what do I do then?"

"Place him in a quiet room, and do not hand him over to anyone but me."

"Begging your pardon, miss, but how do I know you are legit?"

"I can give you the phone number of my supervisor, and Tyler's reaction when he sees me should quell your doubts. Please call Stella, and I'll leave my phone connected to my Bluetooth, but I need to leave now, or Tyler could be at your facility for half the night."

Two and a half hours later, Addison arrived at the station. The officer at the desk barely looked up as he said, "Name?"

Addison answered, and the officer said, "What is your complaint?"

Addison eyed the man and said, "I will complain about you if you continue these stupid questions. Were you not at the desk when I rang first, and you forwarded me to your sergeant? I need to see Sergeant Miles and retrieve my ward."

The young officer blushed and mumbled something. He rang the sergeant, who arrived quickly.

"Miss Bradley, it is good to see you. I spoke to your supervisor, who was most distressed to hear that you were rescuing Tyler from his domestic situation. She said she would talk to you tomorrow, but let's tell Tyler you've arrived."

When Sergeant Miles opened the door and ushered her inside, Tyler had his head on the desk, although Addi didn't think he was asleep.

"Aren't you going to greet me?"

Tyler's head shot up, and he launched himself at Addison.

"Careful, buddy, that belly is not too many doughnuts; it's a baby."

Tyler stepped back. "Uh, sorry. Did I hurt you?"

"No, and I still want a hug."

The police officer watched as Tyler approached Addison cautiously. He smiled when the woman laughed and dragged the boy into her embrace.

"Tye, it's good to see you, but the circumstances aren't the best."

The boy who had held it well together for so many hours burst into tears and sobbed in Addi's arms. The sergeant watched as Addi patted Tyler on the back and made soothing noises. When the boy shuddered and the tears stopped, Addison said, "Thank you for keeping Tyler safe, Sergeant Miles. Just for his peace of mind, can you do a welfare check on his Mother sometime over the next few days."

Sergeant Miles nodded. "I can do that. Go well, young man; what has happened is hurtful, but you have a fierce advocate."

Tyler looked exhausted, so Addison thanked the officer again and led the boy to the car.

" Tye, you can sleep while I drive, talk about what happened while I drive, or eat if we can find a nighttime Maccas. What do you think?"

"Addi, I am starving. Mum stopped buying food, and I had to try begging for stuff from the shop down the road."

"Okay, food first."

A short while later, Addison and Tyley set off again. The shop they found was closing, but the girl in the drive-through window took pity on them. Tyler was eating his second burger, which the staff member made with chicken to accommodate Addison's delicate stomach. They travelled silently as Tyler ate, but Addison knew he would want to discuss what had happened after his meal. She smiled as she realised there would be no talking tonight because Tyler was fast asleep. Addison chuckled as she thought Tye might be in a food coma, but whatever the reason for her companion's sleep, she couldn't begrudge him a peaceful doze.

It was close to two o'clock when Addison pulled into her driveway. Tye woke when the car's motion stopped, and he rubbed his eyes as he tried to focus.

"Bring your bag and come inside. Do you want to shower before you go to bed? I'll put you in the third room because the single in the first room will be too short if you continue to grow."

"Can I have a shower? I know I stink, even if you haven't said anything. I was too scared to shower in case Derek decided to grab me while I was naked."

"Well, Tyler Kendrick, you are safe here, although if you stand in the shower for thirty minutes, I might get a bit testy."

Tyler laughed because that was their argument every morning when he lived here.

While Tyler showered, Addison set her alarm to seven-thirty. By then, someone would be in the office at school, and she intended to take a personal day. Once she had explained what had happened during the night, she knew that her principal would agree to the day without hesitation.

Once Tyler emerged from the shower, Addison said, "I want to know what happened, but I think your explanation can wait until morning. I will stay home with you tomorrow to help you get organised, so you don't need to worry about waking up early. It's nearly three o'clock now, so sleep as late as you like."

Tyson nodded and headed for his bedroom, but before he entered, he said, "Thank you for not questioning me and organising the cops to collect me. This nighttime stuff must be a bother, and I'm sorry."

Addison approached the boy.

"Don't ever apologise for wanting to be safe, and if I had to drive six hours, I would still have come to get you. You, Tyler Kendrick, are important to me, and I'm glad you're here, and I can keep you safe. Now go to bed before we both fall down."

When the alarm sounded, Addison groaned, but hitting the snooze button was not an option. As she listened to the phone ring, she thought about what had happened last night. Although Tye hadn't explained in depth, she had a fair picture of what he had endured. A child who hadn't showered for fear of being cornered was begging for food at a nearby store and wasn't game to sleep because it made him too vulnerable. It spoke volumes for the situation he had found himself in, and Addison was thankful she had provided him with a phone. The staff member who answered the phone at the school was Cathy, and when she heard what Addison was doing that day and why, she was both upset and supportive; she promised to pass the message on to the principal as soon as the woman arrived.

Addison rolled over and went back to sleep after ringing in to take a personal day. When she finally woke, it was close to nine o'clock, and as Addison couldn't hear any noise from Tye's room, she took a quick shower before heading to the kitchen to make breakfast. Tyler stumbled into the kitchen as she poured her tea, rubbing his eyes. Addi smiled affectionately at the boy but said, "Good morning. Are you hungry? I can make eggs on toast if you want; sorry, I have no bacon."

Tye grinned and accepted the eggs on toast option. As she cracked eggs in a bowl, Addison said, "Did you sleep well?"

"Yes. There is nothing to be scared of at your place, so that I can sleep without fear."

"When we finish breakfast, we need to talk. Stella will want to know why I collected you last night and what legal actions we need to take to keep you safe."

"Can you tell me about the baby? You don't have to give me the birds-and-bees talk. I may only be twelve, but I know how it happens. Do you want a baby? Who's the dad?"

"Ah. The dad is the guardian of my last resident. She wasn't a foster but needed a place to live while her newly appointed guardian was overseas with the army. When he returned, he lived here for a few months. He won't be the dad because the baby was an accident, and he doesn't want it, but I do, even if I hadn't planned to have a baby now."

"Wow. Tough luck with the guy."

"Yeah, I thought he was a good guy, but it turns out he's a jerk. Tell me about what happened to you."

Tyeler sat quietly for a moment and then drew a large breath.

"When I went back to live with Mum, everything was good. She went to work and bought food; we got along fine. About six months ago, I went into the lounge room to say good night, and she was smoking a joint. I wanted to cry, but she assured me she could manage a smoke occasionally, which relaxed her after a busy day. I didn't know what to do or whether I believed her, but I didn't say anything. But her occasional became every night, and the food in the fridge dwindled as she spent more money on the weed."

Tye paused his narrative of the past months, then sighed and continued.

"I told her that smoking every night would get her hooked and that we needed the money she spent on drugs for food and bills. Mum said she had a friend who would help pay the bills, and that's when Derek moved in. He was using and dealing heroin, and he started mum sniffing that stuff. Derek was a big, violent bloke. He used to hit Mum most nights, and one day, when he went out, I begged her to leave him, but Mum said she couldn't because she owed him money for the drugs, and he would hunt us down and kill us if we left.

And then, one night, about a week before I called you, Derek offered the drugs to me. I said no; he kept trying to get me to take them, and he laughed, saying I couldn't stay awake forever. He told me I had two choices: sniff the stuff of my own free will, or he'd get me when I least expected, and he'd inject me with the stuff. That's when I called you."

Addison wrapped her arm around Tye's shoulders and hugged him. The retelling of the events leading up to his rescue had unsettled him, and tears welled in his eyes. Addison knew she couldn't save all the kids, but she could keep this one safe.

Chapter Thirteen

After Stella rang and obtained information about the trouble that led to Tyler's removal from his home, she prepared the legal documents that made him a ward of the state. Because of Addison's pleas and the difficulty of placing foster children, the department agreed that the boy should remain with her. After sorting out the legalities, Addison and Tyler headed to the school, where she enrolled him in class, and then visited the second-hand shop for uniforms. Tyler was happy to have second-hand garments after Addison explained that he would be in high school next year and would require a new uniform.

With the school uniforms sorted, Addison took Tyler to a local department store and replaced the tattered garments he had rescued from his house. They visited the local gym where Tyler had previously trained in karate and enrolled the boy in the Monday and Wednesday classes. Addison felt she had done all she could for her new ward, and they went home satisfied. Tomorrow was a new day for Tyler, so after dinner and some reading time, Addison suggested it was bedtime, and Tyler went with a smile.

The following day went well, and Addison congratulated herself on their progress. Tyler arrived at her classroom smiling, and Addison hoped the remainder of his schooling would be enjoyable. After dropping Tyler off at the gym for his karate lesson, Addison went home, planning to make a nice meal for Tyler and herself. Her plans were thrown into disarray after she answered Sergeant Miles's phone call.

"Sergeant Miles, what can I do for you?"

"Miss Bradley, as you requested, we did a welfare check on the house in Burns Street, and unfortunately, the female resident was deceased. We arrested a male who was still as high as a kite, and we are holding him in custody until he is coherent enough to be questioned.

The woman, whom we've yet to identify but assume was Sandra Kendrick, was beaten to death."

"Dear God, what do I tell Tyler?"

"I can't answer that, I'm afraid. We discovered large quantities of cocaine and ecstasy tablets in the house. Even if we can't pin the woman's death on him, he'll go away for a long time on dealing charges."

"Is it likely that he won't face charges for Sandra Kendrick's death?"

"At the moment, he is the only suspect. The evidence all points to him. You might want to tell young Tyler that he couldn't save his Mother, but if she were in her right mind, she would be glad he saved himself. I'll keep in touch when I have more information."

"Thanks, Sergeant Miles."

Addison sat on a chair in the kitchen, all thoughts of the meal she intended to make shrouded by the sadness she would inflict on Tyler.

When Addison picked up Tyler, he was buzzing with excitement about being able to participate in the classes again. Addison suggested he shower while she ordered pizza, and he dashed towards the bathroom, still smiling from his afternoon's enjoyment. Addison was unsure whether to tell Tyler before he ate or afterwards, but he took the decision out of her hands.

"Addi, you've smiled and listened to my stories of how great this afternoon was, but the smile never reached your eyes. Something has happened, and you're afraid to tell me. Please tell me that the department hasn't decided to move me to another placement?"

"Your placement here is permanent, so there is no concern there. You are right about the bad news, and I don't know how to tell you except to say I'm sorry, your Mother is dead."

Tyley didn't say a word, and Addison waited for an emotional outburst, but it never came. Tears leaked from Tyler's eyes, and he said, "So I'm an orphan now? I never had a dad, and my mum didn't care about me enough to stay clean."

"Tye, you might not have those people, but you have me, and I love you like a son."

Tyeler nodded absently. "You know, as horrid as this sounds, she is no longer tormented by the effects of the drugs and her sense of failure when she looks at me. Vets put animals down when they're suffering, but because we are not allowed to do that, the people who suffer have a lifetime of hurt. How did she die?"

"Sergeant Miles says someone beat her to death."

Tyler closed his eyes and clenched his fists.

"And is Derek the suspect?"

"Yes, and apparently, the police turned up a large quantity of cocaine and ecstasy, so he will be charged with that, too."

Tyler gave her a wan smile and said, "Can we eat now?"

During the meal, Tyler spoke of happy memories he and his mother had made, and Addison saw another side of the drug-riddled woman. Tyler seemed to be taking his mother's death better than Addison expected, but she decided to encourage Tye to talk to a counsellor about his turbulent life.

Two unexpected phone calls came one after another one afternoon after school ended for the day. Tye was with the counsellor he had agreed to see, and Addison was taking some time to rest before she had to start meals and other chores. The first call came from Sergeant Miles, and when the man said who he was, Addison tensed, unsure whether the update the man promised would be good or bad.

"Miss Bradley, I'm sorry I've taken so long to update you. The case became more complex than I expected, and the Federal Police became involved because of the drug connection. Our friend Derek seems to have been the bully boy of a drug cartel, and as a result of what happened with the Kendricks woman, the Feds became aware of the connection. But what you and young Tyler want to know is yes, the man is charged with the death of Sandra Kendrick and coupled with his drug and cartel connections, he is never likely to see the world other than through the prison bars. The house is no longer a crime scene, so if Tyler wants items from the house before the bailiffs move in, it would be worth a trip."

"Thank you, Sergeant Miles, for updating me on the outcome of the investigation. I'll check with Tyler about the house."

Addison had barely processed what Sergeant Miles relayed to her regarding the arrests and discovery of drug cartel connections when the phone rang again.

"Hello, I am Victor Lawrence, an attorney at law. The police told me that this was Tyler Kendrick's number. May I please speak to him?"

"Mr Lawrence, Tyler lives at this address, and I am his guardian. What business do you have with a twelve-year-old boy?"

"I beg your pardon; I was unaware that the funeral arrangements for Sandra Kendrick were to be administered by a child. This situation is most awkward."

"As his guardian, I can make decisions on his behalf. What exactly is Tyler supposed to do regarding his mother's funeral?"

When the conversation finished, Addison sat at the kitchen table, sifting through the attorney's information. It appeared that Sanda Kendrick had a funeral plan that she had taken out when Tyler was young, and now she had a substantial amount of money in the fund. Addison decided to discuss this problem with Tye. Still, her suggestion would be to contact an undertaker, specify a cremation using the cheapest coffin and for Tye to scatter her ashes somewhere he thought she would like. The funeral company could pay any surplus funds to Tyler.

With the sadness of Sandra Kendrick's death put behind them, Tye and Addison settled into a comfortable existence. Addison's pregnancy progressed without any problems, and she and Cathy had a well-worked-out plan for future appointments and the upcoming birth. The one positive thing that happened amid all the turmoil was that James had finally completed the documentation required to move

Tammy's body, and he had organised the service at the grave site. During the lengthy process, James remained in Heidelberg, and it appeared to Addison that James and Mrs Francis may have become very fond of each other.

As Addison grew larger, Tyler spent much time fussing over her. He often helped her cook meals and vacuumed because he told her she worked hard enough at school without having to drag the heavy machine around. Addison looked forward to her confinement leave, but as she had booked it to start a week before her due date, she still had a month to endure. Tyler was now riding to his karate lessons, and it was as he entered the house that the phone rang. A man on the other end complained about irresponsible parents, and Tyler couldn't understand the call.

"Addi, can you talk to this man? I don't know what he's talking about."

Addison took the phone from Tyler, and he stood beside her as she tried to make sense of what the man was saying. Eventually, she said, "Sir, if you don't stop cursing and insulting unnamed parents, I will hang up. I assume this call has a point, so get to it."

"Madame, I am at the interstate bus stop where a small unaccompanied child has just alighted. She says her name is Lacey Fisher, and she wishes to be collected."

Addison gasped. "Lacey is there, alone?"

"Yes, madame, and I would appreciate your collecting the child. Babysitting is not in my job description."

"I will come now. It will take me about twenty minutes."

After hanging up the phone, Addison looked stunned.

Tyler collected Addison's bag and car keys and said, "Addi, I don't know who Lacey is, but it seems we need to leave now."

Addison nodded and headed towards the car. As they drove, she told Tyler about Lacey and how she had saved her and the Major when Lacey arrived in Chessberry.

"Is that Lacey's bed in the spare room? Is that why it's a small bed?"

"Yes, to both of those questions. I can't believe Greyson would put her on a bus and send her here unaccompanied. It doesn't make sense."

Addison searched for a park, and when she finally found a space, she and Tyler rushed towards the terminal building.

As Addison opened the door to the office, Lacey raced towards her but stopped when she saw Addison's extended belly.

"Lacey Fisher, come here and hug me before we work out what is happening."

Lacey rushed towards Addison, and her little arms reached around Addison as far as she could.

"I'm not sure if I'm impressed that you made a trip from the other side of the state by yourself or whether I'm appalled. Do you have bags? We need to leave so you can tell me why you're here."

Tye collected Lacey's bag, and Addison thanked the grumpy man for ringing to let her know Lacey was at the terminal.

The trip back was a quiet one after Addison introduced Lacey to Tyler. Addison knew she needed to get to the bottom of the unescorted trip, but she didn't want to overwhelm the child with questions.

Chapter Fourteen

"Tye, we might have take away. Do you want to ring someone to order dinner while I talk to Lacey?"

Addison poured herself a herbal tea and made Lacey her favourite hot chocolate drink. When everyone settled, Addison said, "I need to sort out what happened and why you're here."

Lacey burst into tears, her sobbing tearing at Addison's heart. She collected the sobbing child on her ever-decreasing lap and comforted her until the tears subsided.

"Grey said you didn't ring me because you were busy with other kids and didn't have time for me. Now you have Tyler and the baby, you won't want me, but I can't go back."

Addison raised her eyebrows at Tyler, and he shrugged.

"Lacey, Greyson was wrong. I could have six kids here, and I'd still want you, but I must ask some questions. Does Greyson know you're here?"

"No."

"Okay, give me a minute to call off the search party. Grey has certainly been looking for you, and then you can tell me what happened."

Addison dialled the number for the garrison she used to notify Greyson of her pregnancy. Despite being told he needed to share a number with his family, Greyson had done nothing about it.

"This is Kyana Base. Where can I direct your call?"

"You don't need to direct my call anywhere, but please notify Lieutenant Pellesser that Lacey is with Addison. And the message is urgent because I'm sure Grey will have a search party of thousands looking for his ward."

"I will pass the message on immediately. There is a search party looking for the girl."

Addison disconnected and focused on the hungry children at the table. "Let's eat, and then you can tell me why you are here."

Addison dished their meal, and she and Tye chatted about his karate lesson and the upcoming competition. Tye was excited, and it warmed Addison's heart to hear the excitement in his voice.

Once they finished their meal, Tye organised the clean-up, and Addison took Lacey into the lounge room.

"Lacey, tell me what happened and how you caught a bus halfway across the state."

"I hate living at the base. Greyson always works late, and I have to go to after-school care. I never get to go swimming or go to Guides, and when Grey arrives home, he is tired and grumpy, and all I do is go to bed."

"That doesn't sound ideal, but couldn't you tell Grey how you are unhappy?"

"I can't because he has a lady friend he convinced to look after me when he deploys in a few weeks. Her name is Sandra, and she is horrible. When Grey is around, she is sweet and nice and smiles a lot, but when Grey leaves, she yells at me and tells me what a pest I am. She hits me, and she says that she is Grey's fi-an-ce, and that means they are getting married, and she is going to convince him to send me to boarding school. She said Grey wouldn't believe me that she isn't nice, so there is no point bringing it up because he would be happy to get rid of me after all these years. I know you didn't want to talk to me, but I thought you might make me one of your foster kids, and I could live with you."

" Come here, Lacey."

Addison wrapped Lacey in her arms and said, "The woman is evil."

Setting Lacey on the seat next to her, Addison said, "Let's deal with these untruths one at a time. I don't know why Greyson said I didn't want to talk to you. I rang him and asked him to set up a schedule for FaceTime calls, and he said you had settled well and that seeing me would only upset you. I tried to convince him another day, but he blocked me so that I couldn't call."

"So you wanted to talk to me?"

"Yes. I missed you dreadfully and wanted to hear how you settled in."

"Next thing, I think Grey would listen to you if you complained about the woman, but I can understand why you would be scared. Grey will not send you to boarding school, but if he is deploying soon, you can stay here until he returns. We will sort out who you live with once he's back."

Tye, who had been listening to the conversation, said, "How did you buy a bus ticket, and how did you travel across the state by yourself?"

"I told one of the big girls on the school bus about Sandra. I took Grey's credit card from his wallet, and Heidi bought a ticket online. We skipped school, and she went with me to the terminal. While the driver was loading the bags, Heidi instructed me to head to the back and stay hidden for an hour, as it would be too late to return me to Kyana by then. A nice lady tutted at me when she realised I was alone, but she helped me get to the bathroom and bought me food. I have her name and phone number written down here."

Lacey pulled out an exercise book and handed it to Addison.

Tye laughed. "It's like the plot from a movie."

Addison shook her head.

"Why don't you two get ready for bed? Lacey, use my bathroom. Your room is still the same one you had before; I'll ring this nice lady to thank her and assure her you got home safely."

After her phone conversation with Carol Parkes, Addison checked on the kids. She tucked Lacey in and declined to read a story, thinking Lacey might fall asleep before the first page. Then, she went to talk to Tyler. Addison sat on the bed next to the boy, and he grinned at her.

"She's a pretty brave little kid. I don't think I'd be game enough to do what she did."

"You are right, but dealing with her has made me worry about what happens to you. If the bosses at Child Protection change, they may want to shake things up, and you could get moved."

Tyler went pale and grabbed Addison's hand.

"Please don't let that happen."

"Tye, I've been thinking about an idea I have had for ages since you came back. How would you feel about me adopting you?"

"For real?"

"Yes, for real."

"I would love for you to be my Mum."

"Okay, I'll make enquiries tomorrow, but as exciting as it is, please keep this under your hat. I don't want Lacey to know because she has a guardian who won't take kindly to suggestions that she become my child, and I don't want to disappoint her."

When the phone rang, Addison knew it would be Greyson.

"Let me speak to Lacey."

"Well, hello to you, Greyson. And you are not speaking to Lacey because she is in bed."

"Did you encourage her to do this dangerous trip?"

"Your fiancé prompted the trip. And before I go on, you lying scumbag, you told me you wouldn't marry because you are a career soldier, and within months of arriving at your new post, you are engaged. Why couldn't you find the courage and tell me it was me you didn't want to marry, but your options were open for other women?"

"What rubbish are you talking about, woman? I'm not engaged."

"Your self-proclaimed fiancée, Sandra, told Lacey that you and she would marry and that you would send Lacey to boarding school. Also, the loving, kind front she puts on when you're in the room disappears when you do, and she shouts and calls Lacey names. In addition, she hits Lacey. What were you thinking, bringing a baggage like her into Lacey's life?"

"Why didn't Lacey tell me?"

"Because the woman convinced Lacey, you wouldn't believe her. And from Lacey's description of life on Kyana, it is woeful, considering you work long hours, farm her out on other people and arrive home grumpy and tired."

"How am I supposed to get her back here? I deploy in two weeks, and I don't have time to chase all over the countryside for Lacey."

"Leave her here where she is happy and safe, and we'll talk when you return."

"She has to go to school."

"Send me a document that gives me temporary guardianship, and she can attend school here. Send it by email if you can unblock my address."

"If I ring tomorrow, can I speak to her?"

"Why would I do that when you lied and told her I didn't want to talk to her? But I'm a bigger person and will consider Lacey's wishes. If she wants to talk to you, I will allow it, but as you still have me blocked, you'll have to ring me."

Chapter Fifteen

" Mama Addi, can I go to Guides and go swimming again?"

Addison nodded. She didn't know what to do about Lacey calling her Mama because she felt certain Greyson would be furious and assume she had encouraged the title. If Lacey were to stay for another three months, Addison needed to inform her that when the time came to go to the hospital, James would be the person she called to mind the children while she was away. Lacey hadn't come into contact with the man because he and Mrs Francis had been busy with Tammy's relocation. Tonight would be the first time she had seen the man since she left his home so long ago. While Tyler managed to interact with James, Lacey's aversion to strange men after her association with the man provoked her bereavement.

"Lacey, do you remember the Major?"

Lacey nodded. "He was loud and shouted and bossed me around."

"Yes, he did, which was why I asked to mind you while we waited for Grey to return. He realised how wrong he was to treat you that way and changed how he talked to people. The Major comes to dinner every Thursday night and will be here tonight. Please trust me when I say he will not shout or boss you around. Tyler talks to the man, and I'd like for you to get to know the new him. Can you do that for me?"

Lacey looked nervous but nodded.

"But can I not sit next to him?"

When James walked in, he said, "I took the liberty of inviting someone else."

Addison smiled and said, "Lacey, come out here. There is someone to see you."

Lacey peeked around the kitchen door, and then, with a shout of "Mrs Francis!", she bolted towards the woman. As they laughed and hugged each other, James and Addison watched with huge smiles.

James approached Lacey as the two friends broke apart, saying, "Am I forgiven?"

Lacey nodded shyly, and Addison suggested they take their places at the table as she and Tyler dished the meal. As they neared the end of the meal, James said, "Addison, I wanted to tell you that the project Beryl and I were working on is now complete."

Addison nodded. "You can tell me about that once the kids go to bed."

"The other announcement I must make is that Beryl and I are getting married."

"Oh, my goodness, that is amazing. Congratulations. When is the big day?"

Beryl chuckled. "Can you hold off having that baby for another three weeks? We'll have a small service with a celebrant. We want you there, but my daughter can't get time off until then, so I want to wait for her."

"That makes sense. James, what about your sons? We know Greyson can't come, but you have two others."

James shook his head. "They won't come; we didn't part on good terms, and I doubt they'd want to celebrate my wedding considering how badly I managed my first marriage."

Addison considered his comment but said, "I can't do too much towards the wedding, but I can make a phone call. If you'd like me to try, I can invite them. They can only say no."

"All right, I'll give you phone numbers and see how you go. It's probably well past time to let bygones be bygones."

When Addison told Lacey and Tyler it was time for bed, Lacey asked if Mrs Francis could read her a story. While they were gone, Addison told James that she had adopted Tyler, but they were keeping it quiet for the moment because she didn't want Lacey to decide that was what she wanted.

"No, I can't imagine Greyson would be happy with Lacey changing things. Tammy's internment beside my late wife is complete, and we didn't have a service; we said a few prayers and hoped the ladies could now rest in peace."

The following day, Addison dropped Lacey off at her swimming club, and as Tyler rode his bike to the gym, she had some spare time. She thought there was no time like the present and dialled Nathan Pellesser's work number. The woman who answered the phone sounded young and professional, but balked at Addison's request to speak to Nathan.

"Without an appointment, Mr Pellesser will not see you; he is too busy now."

"I understand that Mr Pellesser might be busy, but this call is about his elderly father, and I doubt he would thank you for blocking me, given that I have information he needs to hear."

"Oh, dear. Give me a moment to speak with him."

The receptionist put Addison on hold, and she listened to the elevator music for longer than she had expected. When the male voice answered the phone and said, "This is Nathan Pellesser. We probably have nothing to say unless you tell me the old curmudgeon is dead."

"Goodness, James said you parted on bad terms, but if you only want to hear that he is dead, I guess we have nothing to discuss. I hope your brother Trent is more receptive."

"Hold on. Is that it? Aren't you going to tell me why you called?"

"Your father has turned over a new leaf. He no longer shouts or issues orders, and he has expressed his remorse for attempting to bully you and your brother into becoming soldiers. He admits that he was an absent father and a lousy husband, but James is getting married in three weeks and hopes you might attend so he can apologise in person."

Addison could hear the sneer in his voice. "Who's he marrying? Some gold digger who's young enough to be his daughter? I don't think so."

"Your father, James, is marrying a fifty-nine-year-old widow who doesn't care if he is rich. She is kind and caring, and they are adorable to watch together."

"What is your part in all this?"

"If you've been in touch with Greyson, you will know he became the guardian of Tammy Fisher's six-year-old daughter. He had deployed when Tammy died and was unable to care for Lacey, so as a registered foster carer, I was able to fill the gap."

"Greyson is the guardian of a little girl? How does that work out? I'm sorry to hear about Tammy."

"We have had some challenges, but Greyson is on deployment again, and Lacey is living with me. What say you, Nathan? Will you and your family attend the wedding?"

"Yes. I'll send you back to my admin, and if you give her the details, we will be there."

Trent Pellesser was more open to the suggestion that he attend his father's wedding when she told him Nathan had agreed. Addison felt satisfied that she had convinced the Pellesser men to attend their father's wedding, and although her increased bulk made other jobs too demanding, the calls she made would help make the wedding a real celebration.

The wedding went off without a hitch, and the guests mingled and chatted during the meal that Cathy and the Ladies' Guild had prepared. Addison made sure to meet Nathan and Trent Pellesser, as well as Nathan's family. Lacey was so excited to discover uncles, an aunt and two cousins. The brothers resembled Greyson, and she was sad that he had missed this celebration. Despite the hostile phone calls, both of James's sons offered their congratulations, and once or twice, when she looked over the crowd, she could see James talking to one of his sons.

Addison had an enjoyable time, but fatigue and discomfort forced her to leave the celebration. When she went to thank James's family for coming, Dianne Pellesser said, "When are you due?"

"Next week. We just got the wedding in before I have my little girl."

Trent said, "It's none of my business, but where is the father?"

"There isn't a father, just a sperm donor. And he's on deployment."

Trent looked shocked, but Nathan said, "Ah, Dad's comment about his granddaughter now makes sense."

Trent said, "He's left you to raise a kid by yourself? I guess I'm not surprised, given his life in the army. I'm surprised he could find time for Lacey."

"Sometimes he can't, which is why she is with me. It's been great meeting you, but I'm tired and need to rest. I hope I see you again."

Tyler rounded up Lacey and Addison's little family and headed to the car. Thankfully, Lacey ran out of energy; excitement and too much food caught up with her, and she went to bed without a complaint. When Addison went in to say good night to Tyler, he said, "You're hurting, aren't you?"

"Yeah. I'll see how long the pains last, but I wouldn't be surprised if little Grace arrives tonight."

Addison thought about her conversation with Tye in the lulls between contractions, never thinking it might be a prophecy. Once she had decided tonight was the night, her planning fell into place. Beryl arrived as Cathy and Austin escorted Addison to the car, but Addison's occasional moans only broke the silence of the drive to the hospital. Baby Grace Elizabeth Bradley arrived in the early hours of Sunday morning. While the midwives cleaned up Addison, they handed Grace to Cathy, and despite her normally stoic character, Cathy cried. This little girl would have all the female support a child should have, and Austin and James would provide the male influence that her absent father would not.

When the staff moved Addison to a room, she fell asleep almost immediately. Meanwhile, Austin and Cathy continued to nurse baby Grace until the nursing staff threw them out. Cathy knew she had a phone call to Addison's parents, who would arrive in a day or two to help Addi cope with a new baby and two excited children. Considering that Beryl had watched the children overnight, the news that Addison had her baby was no secret because once she told James, who had stayed with his sons, he would tell anyone he came into contact with. Beryl smiled. Not only had Addi reconciled with his family, but she had also given him a second granddaughter.

Chapter Sixteen

Two months later

Addison had just settled Grace for a nap when someone knocked on the door. Tyler raced for the door to prevent the visitor from knocking again, knowing full well that Addi needed a respite from her colicky little girl. When he pulled the door open, it was clear who the man dressed in fatigues was.

"Let me get my Mum."

Tyler left the door open and raced towards the nursery.

"Mum, there's a man at the door. I think it is that guy Greyson."

Addison sighed. "Go and ask him to come in, but give me a minute to tidy up. Could you put the kettle on?"

Addison's eyes zeroed in on the tall man pacing the floor in the lounge room. He seemed larger than she remembered, and the beard he wore the last time she saw him was missing. She had to admit it was a crime to camouflage that square jaw and the dimple under his mouth.

"For goodness' sake, Greyson, sit down. Tye is making a drink if you want something."

"Who's the boy, and where is Lacey?"

"I don't remember you being rude and abrupt before. It seems that the army is turning you into a neanderthal. The boy is Tyler, my son, and Lacey is at Guides. Maybe if you collect her in an hour, she will be excited, making her homecoming quieter."

"Why does she have to be quiet?"

"Because Grace is unsettled, and I've just put her down, and Lacey can talk so loud she wakes Grace."

"Who the hell is Grace, and why is she sleeping?"

Addison shook her head. "Grace is my daughter, and if you are going to be unpleasant, I suggest you go to your Father's rather than sit here. But you'd better watch your manners because your father won't let you be rude to Beryl."

"And Beryl is....?"

"His wife. You were out of the country, and I'm tired of talking to that corporal at the reception desk. Your brothers, Nathan's wife, and kids came to the wedding. It was a small turnout, and everyone enjoyed themselves."

"You have a son and a baby, and my father has a wife. Have you all gone mad?"

"No. It's called living, something you don't do in the army. You go from point A to point B, then they send you overseas, and when you return, you resume your routine. There's no time in there for unscheduled living. Do you want a drink, or are you leaving?"

As she asked the question, Tye arrived with a steaming mug and handed it to Addi. He placed a plate of biscuits on the coffee table and looked at Greyson.

"Can I get you something, Lieutenant Pellesser?"

"Thanks, I'll have whatever Addi is having.

Tyler and Addison laughed, and Addi said, "Ah, maybe not. Tye laced my tea with Guinness; it's supposed to help with breastfeeding. Tye, get Greyson a white coffee."

Greyson took the cup, and after a sip, he said, " Why are you so damned happy?"

Addison smiled. "I have my son, my daughter and Lacey; I have support from my parents and your entire family, and I have Cathy and Austin. Why wouldn't I be happy?"

"Well, I'm going to rain on your parade because I've come to get Lacey."

"Will making a little girl unhappy justify your existence? Tammy may have chosen you as Lacy's guardian, but she would have looked for an alternative if she knew how that worked out. Why do you want to take her back to Kyana? Lacey hates it there; she doesn't see enough of you, can't go swimming or to Guides, and spends most of her life at school or after-school care."

"I am her guardian and will take her with me when I go."

"You'd better go now, or you will be late picking her up. Are you eating with us or not?"

"Yeah, I want to spend as much time with Lacey as possible before we head home."

An hour later, when there was no sign of Greyson and Lacey, Addison began to worry.

Tyler voiced her concerns."Do you think he never intended to come back here? Do you think he is halfway to Kyana?"

Addison brushed the tears from her eyes. "That's what I'm worried about. I might ask John if they have seen Greyson and Lacey."

When Greyson's father hadn't seen him, it further confirmed Addison's fears that Greyson had kidnapped Lacey and headed for his base. They had waited long enough for Greyson and Lacey to return; if they had waited much longer, the meal would have spoiled. Addison knew Tye would not eat unless she did, and the growing boy needed his food. Addison tried to chat about Tye's upcoming test to gain his green belt, and for a while, she was able to push her fears aside. Tye was so excited by his progression that it would be churlish to overshadow his joy with fears about Lacey.

As Tye prepared for bed, he could hear Addison crooning at Grace in the nursery, and his sadness overwhelmed him. Lacey was such a spunky kid, and Greyson Pellesser's decision to remove her from a loving home and place her in a sterile base was just wrong. He turned on his bedside light and flicked off the overhead light when he heard the unmistakable sound of Lacey's voice. Tye walked along the hallway and encountered Greyson and Lacey as they headed for her bedroom. Tye felt furious, and for the first time, he ignored Lacey and stalked towards the nursery. Addison was seated in her rocking chair, feeding Grace.

"Mum, they are home."

Addison nodded. "I can't bear to look at Greyson or to hear Lacey's excited chatter. When she is in bed, can you tell him to go?"

"It will be my pleasure."

Greyson strolled into the kitchen and smiled at Tyler.

"How's it going, mate?"

"You need to leave. Addi doesn't want to talk to you."

"What's her problem?"

Tyler rolled his eyes. "You are supposed to be a smart man; what do you think her problem is? How do you think Addi felt when you were supposed to be here for dinner and didn't show up? We were convinced you had kidnapped Lacey and were halfway to Kyana. Addison is a great mum, and you intend to take Lacey to a place she hates just because a woman who no longer knew you thought you'd be honourable and would do the right thing by her daughter."

"That's enough. You know nothing about my relationship with Lacey and Addison."

"I'm not stupid. I know you and Addi had a relationship, and you didn't want the baby—way to go, soldier, serving your country and avoiding your responsibilities in the real world. Is the army full of men like you? Leave Addi alone; all you do is cause her grief and heartache. You might be able to turn off your emotions, but she can't."

Greyson looked at the fierce determination on the young man's face and sighed.

'I never meant to hurt her."

"Well, you did, so get out of here before she comes into the kitchen and has to see you."

As Greyson nodded and walked away, Addi walked into the kitchen.

"Thank you for having my back. I heard and appreciated much of what you said, but I never wanted to get you tangled up in this mess."

"Mum, I'd rather be tangled up here with you than be anywhere else."

Greyson sat in his car in the driveway of his Father's house. Could he ask His father or Beryl for advice? Grey wanted to take Lacey when he returned to Kyana because he felt lonely amongst the hundreds of men around him. Was he being selfish to take her away from all she had here? The things Tyler said about his treatment of Addi and Grace stung because they were true. He extracted himself from the small compact he had bought when he had arrived in Chessberry and headed for the house. When he walked in, his father glared at him.

"Well, thank goodness you didn't kidnap Lacey and head for Kyana with her. Do you know how worried we were when you disappeared with her?"

Greyson held up his hands to stop his father's tirade.

"I have already had to listen to Tyler giving me a lecture; I don't need another one. What I do need is advice."

Beryl nodded. "I can see that you are confused, but for interest's sake, where did you and Lacey go?"

"Lacey wanted pizza for tea. I told her Addi had cooked dinner, but she still wanted pizza, and I didn't want to disappoint her. While getting our food, she saw a poster promoting the circus that arrived in town and begged me to take her. I knew it was unlikely that Addi could manage a circus visit with a small baby, so we went."

"And it never occurred to you that Addi would be worried? You couldn't text her a message to allay her fears?"

Greyson looked at the woman who was now his stepmother.

"Ah, no, it didn't occur to me. When I lived here, I would take Lacey away for the weekend, and we never had to report our whereabouts or arrival time to Addison."

"Son, I was a lousy husband and an absent father, and it's taken me till I'm sixty to work out what is vital in life. Just because you treated Addison like she didn't count after you arrived to woo Lacey doesn't mean it was right then, and it isn't right now."

Beryl said, "What did you want to seek advice about?"

Greyson related his conversations with Addison and Tyler about Lacey's support system here in Chessberry.

"Is it wrong to take Lacey back to Kyana with me?"

Silence met his question until Beryl said, "Remind me, Greyson, how did Lacey get to Chessberry?"

He shrugged. "On the bus."

"Do you think a child who travels halfway across the state by herself to reach Addison is someone who wants to return to Kyana?"

A sigh was the only answer Greyson could make. After Tyler's lecture, he had a fair indication that taking Lacey to Kyana was a lost cause.

"I miss her when she isn't there."

"I'm sure you do, but is that reason enough to torture the child?"

"No, you're right. I'll talk to Addi to make the arrangements before I speak to Lacey tomorrow."

Greyson rang Addison the following morning to check her schedule. He needed to talk to her without distractions, although if the baby wasn't asleep, that might spoil his plans. When he arrived just before lunch, as Addison had suggested, he scrutinised the woman who was the mother of his baby. He guessed Addison had gained weight during her pregnancy, but she was in good shape two months after the birth.

Lunch was a little awkward, and neither was willing to broach the subject of last night's excursion. Addison left the dishes in the sink and ushered Greyson to the lounge room, where they could sit more comfortably.

"Last night, I got a lecture from Tyeler and one from my Father. Lacey wanted pizza, and while we were at the shop, she saw the circus poster. I thought that was something you couldn't do with a tiny baby, so we went. When I lived here, it was the kind of thing I used to do, so it didn't occur to me that I needed to check in with you."

"For your information, your Father and Beryl were taking Lacey to the circus and wanted to surprise her with the trip. And because you treated me like the housekeeper when you first moved here, you thought it was okay to ignore my feelings again. Did it never occur to you that, having been Lacey's sole parent for over three months, I might have enjoyed some outings? I knew the purpose was to get Lacey used to you, so time alone was necessary, but it hurt my feelings that you never wanted me there. Last night, when you didn't come back, it was terrifying. The thought that you had left without her belongings and without letting her say goodbye was heartbreaking."

Greyson stood and paced the room. Addison could tell he was angry, but so was she.

"Why would everyone think I would kidnap Lacey and leave without letting her say goodbye?"

"Maybe because those are the vibes you give off."

"Well, for your information, I decided it would be better for Lacey if she remained here. But I want phone calls and video chats because I will miss her."

Addison snorted. "You should be grateful that I am more honourable than you, and I will let her talk to you. It might be wise to give me a phone number I can call because talking to the corporal at the desk is overrated."

Lacey cried when Greyson left, but despite her sadness at losing him, she never wanted to go to Kyana base, so the decision to continue living with Addison suited her well.

Epilogue

As the weeks passed, the number of phone calls and video chats between Lacey and Greyson declined. For weeks, Greyson made no contact with his ward, and Addison became concerned about his welfare. A man who lived with his ward and grew to love her would not cease contact unless there was a problem. Addison waited until Lacey went to bed and rang the number Greyson had given her. When it went to message bank, she left a non-confrontational message and waited for a response. Two days later, when Greyson rang Addison, he was abrupt, and it was clear he didn't want to talk.

"What do you want, Addison?"

"Oh, so many things. I want to know why you no longer contact Lacey, who is most upset and wonders if I have done something to stop you from ringing her. I want to know why you're so angry that I contacted you, and I'm worried about you. What is going on, Grey?"

Addison heard the sigh over the phone and wondered whether Greyson would answer or end the call.

"Addi, I have some tough decisions to make, and my free time is filled with confusion, worry and a tinge of fear. I miss you and Lacey, but involving you two in my decision-making process will only make it harder to make an informed choice. Tell Lacey I miss her, but the phone calls must stop now. I will tell her what I have been doing the next time I see her."

"Okay, I don't exactly understand, but stay safe. I'll tell Lacey that you miss her and that you will see her when you have free time. Did you get the invitation to Cathy and Austin's wedding?"

"Yeah, I should be able to make it. I'll email my acceptance when we finish here."

When Addison hung up, she didn't feel better about what was happening with Greyson than before the call. While Greyson may have confided in her at the beginning of their relationship, now he kept everything to himself. Addison didn't have the spare time to worry about Greyson. Raising three children without a husband was tricky, but she was grateful for the support of her friends and relations.

As Cathy and Austin's wedding approached, Addison had to find the time to plan Cathy's bachelorette party and squeeze in appointments to alter her dress as she continued to lose weight. Lacey was beside herself because Cathy had asked her to be a flower girl, and she got to wear a beautiful dress with lots of ruffles, which Lacey loved. Greyson had responded positively to the invitation, but as the guests began to arrive, no one had sighted him. Just as she was ready to head up the aisle, a murmur went through the crowd, and Addison craned her neck to see what was happening. Greyson made his way towards the seats where his father and stepmother sat, but the reason for the comments was that Greyson was in full dress uniform. Cathy's sister fanned herself and said, "Oh, my God. Get a look at him. I might have to make his acquaintance once the reception begins."

Addison felt a surge of jealousy rush through her, but she smiled bravely and tried to remember that Greyson wasn't hers, and she doubted he ever had been.

The wedding went off perfectly; the vows were touching, and the couple's adoration for each other was evident. Once the speeches were over and the dancing began, Addison had to have her first dance with Austin's grabby brother, Vince. Despite Addison moving his hands to the proper position for the waltz, his hands continued to roam. Thankfully, when the dance ended, Addison hurried away in search of Tye for the next dance. Her son blushed, but, as she had taught him to dance — especially for the wedding — he did an excellent job guiding Addison through the following few dances.

Addison sent Tye to ask Beryl if she wanted to dance and looked around for John. Despite trying not to notice Greyson, ignoring him was hard as he and Cathy's sister danced dance after dance. She caught his eye and looked away hurriedly, but he walked across the floor towards her when the dance finished.

"Will you dance with me?"

"I thought you might be too tired to dance; you've been quite the spectacle partnering Joyce on the dance floor."

"Please, Addi, don't give me a hard time. I want to dance with my girls, so when you and I finish, I will dance with Lacey."

Greyson held out his hand for Abbi, and she placed her hand on his.

"You look beautiful today."

"Thank you, but you caused quite a stir when you walked into the church in your dress uniform. It occurred to me that I have seen you in fatigues but never in your dress uniform. You look very handsome."

The music slowed, and Greyson pulled Abbi into his arms. This close, she could smell his body wash and the clean smell of his uniform. Tucked against him, Addison sighed; how could he still affect her after all the hurt he had caused her?

"What are you thinking?"

"I'm wondering why I never got over caring for you. After all the horrid things you said and did, I should hate you, but I don't."

"May I cut in?"

Addi looked over Greyson's shoulder and saw Vince standing there with a smile. As Greyson looked at her, Addison shook her head and said, "No. You may not cut in. Find someone else to dance with."

"Don't be a spoilsport, sweetheart. Let the other girls drool over the pretty soldier and come and dance with me."

Greyson practically growled. "The lady said no, so go and dance with someone else."

Vince walked away with a scowl directed at both Greyson and Addi, and she sighed.

"He is going to make tonight unpleasant. I've danced the regulation dances with him, but he is handsy, and I don't want to be mauled by him."

Greyson snarled. "Fucker," he said. "Come and dance with my Dad while I dance with Lacey. Tell Dad you don't want to dance with the man, so if he tries to cut in, Dad should refuse."

Dodging Vince became a full-time job, and Addison was glad when Cathy asked her to help her change before the married couple left for their honeymoon. As Addison helped Cathy remove the voluminous dress, Cathy grinned and said, "Vince seems smitten with you. He asked me all about you and whether you had a partner. You know you could do worse."

"Cathy, I love you and don't want to offend, but after the first few dances where Vince spent the entire time feeling me up, I have avoided him. You're right. I could do worse, but that doesn't mean I would settle for a handsy predator."

"Oh, my gosh. We are leaving, and even if I tell Austin to tell his brother to leave you alone, what happens after we leave?"

"Stop worrying. After you leave, Lacey, Tye and I will leave. Lacey is already yawning, and considering Mrs Fields has Grace, I need to relieve her of that responsibility."

After the hugs, kisses and well wishes, a driver whizzed them away in a limousine. No sooner had the newly married couple left than Vince approached Addison.

"Sweetheart, why don't you have a nightcap with me? I have a room upstairs where we could relax."

Addison pasted on a fake smile and said, "That is so generous, but I need to collect my kids; it's past their bedtime."

"Kids? What kids?"

"The flower girl is mine, the handsome young man over there with the elderly couple is mine, and the baby is at home with a sitter."

At the appalled look on Vince's face, Addison felt like laughing. Then Vince laughed. "Ah, you had me going for a second."

Addison called Tye, and when he approached, she asked him to check that Lacey hadn't fallen asleep in a corner because they were ready to go.

"Sure, mum, I know where she is."

If Vince thought she was teasing him, Tye's comment provided all the proof he needed to believe she was a mother with three children.

"Um, it was nice to meet you, Addison. Thank you for being my partner."

As they walked towards the entrance, Tye, carrying a sleepy Lacey, Greyson stepped up.

"Do you want me to take her?"

Tye waited a moment and said, "Sure. Thanks, she's a heavy little thing when she's asleep."

Greyson placed Lacey in the car and kissed her on the forehead,

"Can I call tomorrow? I have some things to tell you."

"Sure. Tye is playing golf with your father, and Lacey is cooking with your Mum, so we will only have Grace as a distraction. She usually sleeps around ten, so come then."

The following day, the Bradley household got a late start, so by the time John and Beryl arrived to collect the kids, it was almost ten o'clock. Greyson arrived with his parents, and despite Lacey's cajoling, he refused to bake cakes with his mom because he had a meaningful conversation with Addi. Lacey accepted with bad grace, and he told her that if she sulked, he wouldn't take everyone out for dinner. With the prospect of spending more time with Grey, Lacey conceded.

"Come into the kitchen. Thank heavens Grace went down without a fuss, because Lacey was already tired and cranky, even before you refused to bake cakes with her. I need a drink; do you want one?"

Greyson nodded absently, and when Addison handed him the drink, he nervously cleared his throat.

"Please be patient; I have a lot to tell you."

"Okay."

"When we were kids, Dad dragged us around base after base as he chased promotion. It wasn't until I met Tammy that I had a real friend, but Dad moved us on, and she and I were heartbroken. Friendships with the opposite sex are unusual when you are nine or ten, but Tammy saw me. Eventually, Mum got tired of starting again in a new town and moved us back to Warburton, where I reconnected with Tammy. We were inseparable until I went into the army. Tammy tried to convince me that following my father's dream wouldn't make me happy, but I had no job aspirations and thought I might as well make Dad proud of me."

"And your brothers refused to be swayed by John's wish, so as his last son, you joined up."

"Yes. When it came time to re-up, I signed on for another six years, and after watching how my parents' marriage worked and my mates' marriages disintegrated, I decided I wouldn't marry. I had no skills I could use in civilian life, so I intended to be a lifer. But then I got a letter from a woman I didn't know, and my whole world changed. Initially, I could have fobbed Lacey off onto someone else, but after those video calls, I grew to love her, which I suppose was your intention. You intrigued me, and when I met you, I knew you would be trouble."

Greyson stopped, but Addison thought he was gathering her thoughts, not waiting for questions, and when he resumed, she knew she had guessed right.

"I fell in love with you, but that didn't fit in my life plan, so when the army transferred me, I tried to block you out, which spectacularly backfired on me. I was struggling with how to have you in my life when you broke the news that you were pregnant, and I panicked. I said horrible things and acted like a jackass. Lacey ran away to live with you, and I knew I had to re-evaluate my lifestyle if I wanted to include the two females essential to my happiness."

Greyson took Addison's hand.

"I'm sorry for taking you for granted, for causing you heartache, and for suggesting you terminate your pregnancy. I've caused you grief and let you down, and as much as I regret my behaviour, I can't take all the bad things away. Please forgive me, but I know I must earn your forgiveness. I vow to do the best I can. If you ever forgive me, I want to be in your life and in Lacey, Grace, and Tyler's lives. When I stopped ringing you, I struggled with whether I wanted you guys more than the security of army life. You won. I hope you got a picture of me in my dress uniform because it will be the last time you see me in uniform; I have formally resigned. I am now a civilian."

Greyson didn't know if the stunned look on Addison's face was a good thing or a bad thing.

"Addi, say something."

"You want me, Lacey, Grace and Tye, so you quit the army."

"Yes."

"You said you loved me; do you still have feelings for me?"

"Yes."

Are you going to live in Chessberry?"

"Yes, I am, and hopefully, we will live as a family someday. I want you —the kids, the school runs, and all the other things that make up family life. I see how happy Dad is with Beryl, and I don't want to wait until I'm sixty to find happiness when it's right in front of me. Denying the connection between us would be a foolish move, and while I may be a jackass, I'm not a fool."

"Last night, I said I never got over caring for you, and while I want to return to where we were, I can't. It will take some time not only to desire you but also to trust you. I want everything you want, but please understand that we have been together without you for a long time, so reintegrating you might take time and patience. Tye will be the most complicated person to sway because he has supported me for the last few years."

"I understand and am grateful that he looked after you. I would never diminish the connection between you two, but if I eventually move back in here with you, I want to be able to sleep without fearing he might stab me."

Addison chuckled. "That won't happen."

The sound of a baby crying ended their conversation.

"Addi, I will leave now, but I promise I will be back. Can I kiss you before I go?"

Addison stepped closer to Greyson and tilted her head. He needed no more invitation than that, and as he kissed her gently, the crescendo of the wails increased. Greyson shook his head and laughed.

"I guess I will have to fit my kisses in with the needs of the hungry. Go before Grace dies of starvation, but be warned, there will be many more kisses."

Addison smiled. "I'll look forward to that."

Don't miss out!

Visit the website below and you can sign up to receive emails whenever Robyn C Rye publishes a new book. There's no charge and no obligation.

https://books2read.com/r/B-A-FKBW-UXJID

Also by Robyn C Rye

Farnsworth Sisters
Marrying a Rogue
Rescuing Hannah

The Buckingham Sisters
Lady Maggie's Challenge
Layla's Unwanted Husband

The Evans Family
Sometimes Love is not Enough
Still the One
Moving Forward

Standalone
One More Chance
Lady Jayne's Reputation
Third Time's the Charm
Can't Stop Loving You

The Marriage Scam
An Unlikely Match
Searching For You
The Unexpected Suitor
The Lady and the Duke
Starting Over
An Unforgettable Stranger
The Duke's Revenge
The Temporary Wife
Against The Odds
Betrayed
No Good Turn Goes Unpunished
Lady Eloise's Soldier
Lillian's Forbidden Beau
Remember Me
Always Second Best
When One Door Closes
Coming Home to You
Chasing Shadows
Fool Me Once
Deserting Lady Audrey
My Unlikely Saviour
Lies and Deception
A New Beginning
Julia's Second Chance
The Hidden Enemy
The Maiden's Redemption
Miss Elizabeth's Season